BONDS OF ASCENSION

A WEAVERS OF DESTINY NOVELLA

ANDREW PLATTEN

Dedication

Writing and publishing the first book in the Weavers of Destiny series, Strands of Time and Magic, was a journey full of fun, challenges, and plenty of nerve-wracking moments. There were also welcome surprises—friends and family offered amazing support, and receiving positive reviews from readers I had never met was incredibly encouraging. To all the readers who share their enjoyment of the story, it's hard to express just how much it means to an author.

The publishing and marketing side was more complex than I expected. Along the way, though, I discovered an amazing community of indie fantasy writers and readers who warmly welcome new authors and offer invaluable advice. For those unfamiliar, 'indie' refers to independently published authors, a growing and influential force in the fantasy genre.

Your collective support inspires me to keep writing, and for that, I sincerely thank you.

Note to Reader:

Bonds of Ascension is a companion novella to the Weavers of Destiny series and can be enjoyed at any time—whether before, after, or alongside the main books.

Please note that this book follows British spelling and grammar conventions, reflecting the author's British heritage.

Thank you for your understanding. Happy reading!

MORDELAND

BACKALAR

NORTHERN REGION

Dynos

Sandrick

THE HAC

MOBI

YARROW

RAILE

NUULAN

Matalon

Harding
Estate

SOLARYTH

ROSTAL

QUARTT

LANTHE

CAVERN

Haxley

Plainhand
Estate

Troll

RAINBOW
ARCHIPELAGO

Chapter One

Tekira wiped her brow before the sweat dribbled into her eyes. It was not the desert's fierce heat making her perspire, but fear. The angry horde of two hundred villagers had covered half the distance from the mountain that had obscured their approach. She had scant minutes to act. The mob moved with grim determination, pitchforks held low—their energy too precious to waste until they closed the gap.

She pushed her daughter deeper into the crevice the drought had widened over recent weeks. Ripping three withered branches off a dying bondaberry bush, she camouflaged the opening.

They won't hurt a child. They won't!

Tekira's bond-mate rode the air currents high above, sending images of the approaching throng and increasingly ardent warnings that it was time to depart.

Guya, fly fast to Sofi. Bring help, Tekira sent over their mental connection. It would take the goshawk ten minutes to fly to the adjacent fields where several warriors tended crops. It would take twice that for them to run to their aid; that's if they understood the reason for her prida's arrival, and if they were not embattled themselves. She needed to stall for time. The clan would expect a defence, even against such odds. Running was her last resort.

The seasons had warmed rapidly over the last few cycles. Food had always been scarce in the arid climate, but now it was becoming impossible to farm. At last year's Gathering ceremony there had been talk of becoming less isolationist. The idea of trading with the lush northern lands and offering mercenary services in exchange for coin to procure food was gaining popularity. Everyone wanted to be at this year's Gathering to vote, which is why Tekira guarded the plot alone, and Sofi and three workers guarded the adjacent oasis. They would vote later when relieved by others.

No attack had been expected, despite the tensions the drought conditions had wrought. It was a shocking testament to how desperate the clan's neighbours had become.

"I can fight with you, Mama," Lu's determined voice called up from the hole at Tekira's feet.

"No, little warrior, there are too many to fight. But you are brave, and I love you. This mob is starved and angry. I will use wise words to slow them. My sword will be a last resort." She pushed her hand down through the branches and gently touched Lu's head. She fought to keep her tone level.

"You know how we play the game of ghosts, little one?"

"I keep silent and slow my heart and my breath. I still my blood so not even a ghost can hear me. Then I strike with my sword from the shadows."

"Yes, but today's game is different. Today's lesson is to close your eyes, and no matter what you hear, hide from the ghosts until you hear from one of the clan. Can you do that?"

"Yes, Mama." Tekira felt Lu's head tip back and forth in a solemn nod—so typical of her six-summers-old daughter. She held the vivid image her memory gave her firmly in her mind.

"Are you scared, Mama?"

"Mobi'dern don't fear, my little warrior," said Tekira. This time, she had to wipe away a tear. She used her other hand, not wanting to withdraw her touch from her daughter's brow. "Good, then show me—" She had been about to add "and make me proud," but her throat clenched, and she choked down a sob instead. With a last loving squeeze, she tore her hand away and stood.

Tekira jogged to meet the seething mass and noted with relief, they slowed at her approach.

Fear. Determination. Hunger. Their starved faces bore gaunt expressions. Their bodies were thin and hunched. They wanted this even less than she did. But they had families of their own to feed, and the clan had treated them harshly when they sent raiders or ambassadors in the past.

Our isolationist ways will haunt us—we should have helped them.

Meeting the raiders fifty strides from the oasis to negotiate *might* slow them down, and the distance would dull the sound of death to Lu's small ears if it did not.

"Hold, halt," Tekira said in the firm voice she typically used to command her fighting unit. She held her arms out, away from the deadly blade in its scabbard on her back. When the crowd kept coming, she tried a softer tone. "Let us talk. I have permission to share our crops." They did not slow down. Their eyes were fixed on the field, except for the occasional glance her way.

"Who among you has the authority to negotiate? The price will be fair and only due after the rains fall."

Whether they understood it was a delay tactic or were too hungry to reason she did not know, but the mob suddenly quickened their pace. She drew her blade and fell into First Stance, left foot forward, right heel angled to it, knees bent, sword high over her head pointing backwards.

The mob shifted; they had obviously practiced their maneuver, and twenty sharp pitchforks lifted to meet her. Tekira could probably kill these twenty, but beyond the desperate faces, she saw a hundred more closing in. She worried that provoking them would neither spare her daughter nor protect the crops.

"Halt your attack. We all know two hundred will defeat one, but I vow to take twenty of you with me to a sandy grave. Stand down, and your brothers and sisters will live, and be fed." Tekira saw through Guya's eyes as he neared Sofi's plot. They were not under attack, and she had three warriors with her. That might be enough. At her urging, the goshawk arrowed downwards, keening loudly as it approached.

A big man with a long beard to her left lunged, the sharp prongs aimed at her stomach. She whipped her blade downwards, severing the shaft of his pitchfork. His boldness triggered a teen to her right to strike. He gave away his intent when he pushed an older woman— his mother Tekira guessed—protectively behind him. Tekira whipped her blade obliquely across her body at head height; an ineffective strike, but the whistle it made intimidated the boy and crowd to step back. To her sides, the mob continued, encircling her. Several others broke off, running for the field, now she was trapped.

The teen's rusted tines gleamed menacingly in the morning light, their jagged tips blunt, but eager for her flesh. She heard, more than saw another man thrust at her back, just as the teen pressed forward. She turned sideways, allowing the vicious blade of the attacker's hoe to skim under her arm. She drew her elbow back, smashing the man's nose.

A shocked gurgle refocused her on the teen. The hoe's rough-hewn cutter had been sharpened to a wicked edge. It clanged off the teen's wooden shaft, deflecting up into the boy's neck. He grabbed at it, his eyes and mouth wide. As the crowd gasped, Tekira lowered her stance and took four long steps, each in a different direction. Her blade flashed out each time, slicing through a foot, a calf muscle, a thigh, and a kneecap. As men cried out in agony, she whipped her blade through the air several times, trying to cow the mob.

"Won't you stop? You are killing yourself!" she yelled. The big man with the severed shaft held his hand high, attempting to gain the attention of his companions.

He is their leader. Tekira pivoted to face him, keeping her blade up. She kept her head side on, so she could watch the boy on the ground, his mother and others attempting to save him. Her heart went out to them; it could be her daughter, just fifty strides away.

"You Mobis haven't traded with us for months. Why should we believe you will give us food now? It's a ploy to save your own life," the big man spat. Tekira turned her head, squaring off fully with him.

"But my life isn't at risk," she replied. "I can't kill you all, but I can kill enough to cut a path and run." Her level tone caused him to ease back, his mind clearly racing to decide the best course.

"But will the clan honour your words?"

"There's a vote today. You know that already, or you wouldn't have picked today for your raid. There will be new leadership. We are sick of this, too. Many of us see a better way."

"But this is our one chance. If we leave now, and the vote goes different, we starve." Tekira was optimistic about the vote, but she understood the man's fear.

"A compromise? Each of you take just a small amount. Not enough for the clan to want revenge, but enough to keep you going. Take that, and your injured, and your lives." She put every ounce of emotion and belief into her plea, her mind split between the man and Lu, hidden deep in the earth, close by. Was she risking too much? There was still time to run, collect Lu, and escape. Her mind reeled. She did not lack courage for herself but was terrified she had made a grave miscalculation about her daughter's safety.

Through Guya's eyes she saw Sofi look in her direction, recognition lighting her face. She heard the cry of battle and saw the four warriors sprinting. An eagle took to the sky, and two wolves and a large cat bounded her way. Her thoughts raced as she calculated the time it would take for help to arrive. She stared hard at the man leading the mob. He was terrified too, trying to come to his own conclusion. *What else could I offer? Or should I take a more aggressive tack? Is Lu disciplined enough to stay hidden? Have I done what the clan expects?* Her mind reeled, distracted. She had never faced such a personal dilemma.

The nudge on her back brought her back. It felt just like a bump, but then the pain ripped through her. She looked down to see bloody prongs poking out through her chest like angry fingers. She tried to turn her body, but it would not respond; only her head swiveled. The boy's mother held the shaft, her eyes wet and livid, a vicious snarl gripped her mouth.

"My boy–" was the last sound Tekira heard as her body began to shut down, and her knees gave way. Her final thoughts were of

Guya's scream and of the little warrior she would never see challenge the trials, and never see bond with her prida.

Deep in the crevasse, Lu stilled her body, blending in with the rock and sand. She tried to focus on the mantra she had been taught, but every sound from above yanked her mind back to the surface. She was only six, but warrior enough to picture the battle unfolding above her. She would honour her mother's last instruction and hide from the ghosts until Sofi arrived. Then she would live with other ghosts for the rest of her life.

Chapter Two

Nine years later

Lu took a sip from her waterskin and then poured the remainder over her head to cool off. She was careful to lean forward to prevent any liquid from spilling onto her neck or back, where it would dribble down between her leathers and her skin. Any chafing would be distracting during the next leg of their run. She knelt by the river, refilled the bladder, attached it to the clips on her harness, and then picked up the large roll of leather by its shoulder straps. She lifted the bundle onto her back and checked the buckles once more to ensure its weight was evenly spread across her broad shoulders.

Jorak and Nytis were settling their own leather rolls onto their backs, but Dayla was struggling with hers. Nytis stepped forward to help, but Relik stopped her with a sharp hand signal. Dayla was four years their senior, and this was probably the last season the clan would entertain her as a warrior candidate.

She's determined enough, but her body lacks the ability to retain enough muscle, Lu thought. She felt sympathy for the girl, but her nose wrinkled at the thought of a warrior accepting help for something as simple as hoisting her pack. *At least she has her Star Stone.*

Each warrior candidate took turns leading the group cross country towards Mobi, and Dayla would take point for the next five bells. She had already secured three of the four warrior pins required to enter the trials, including the Star Stone awarded for feats of long-distance travel, living off the land, and navigational prowess. Lu had obtained her own on her first attempt last year, travelling solo from Mobi to the nation's capital, Nuulan, in twelve days. Not a record for a novice, but a time of which she was proud.

When Dayla's pack was settled, she took time to ensure the rest of her equipment was correctly secured, then led the group southeast at a slow run. Lu settled into fourth place, having just relinquished the lead spot. Relik, their teacher for this trip and a fully fledged Mobi'dern warrior, took up the rear.

"Take the northern road," Relik called ahead. "Falli reports the pass is clear of spring snow." Lu greatly respected the warrior but thought an owl an odd choice for a prida. She knew it was always the animal who chose, initiating the bond during the days of the communion, but still, an owl did not seem as useful as other pridas.

Relik was the senior apprentice to the Forge—the member of the Council of Old Women in charge of the production of armour and weapons. An owl seemed too timid a companion for one so important. Lu hoped an eagle would choose her when the time came. The great raptor, Mowry, if she was lucky. Being chosen by one of the best prida was crucial to elite status and the fast-track benefits it brought.

Lu enjoyed the north, but she looked forward to arriving home, partly because she missed the daily training, but also because she could begin to turn the leather in her bundle into her Mobi'dern armour. If she passed the trials later this year, she wanted the traditional clothing ready.

Decades ago, this trip would have neither been required nor desired. There had been sufficient clean water to breed cattle and complete the tanning process. Then each successive season brought increasing heat. Today, there was plenty of water in the underground streams, but insufficient wood for the fires required to purify enough water for crops, animals, and the clan.

Lu's chest tightened as memories of her mother's death surfaced. Over time, the pain had dulled enough for her to recognise two positives that emerged from Tekira's sacrifice, though her heart still burned with anger.

The first benefit was the impact on her own life. The clan's harsh existence produced many orphans, who were raised by the all-female community in a communal family. In Lu's case, her mother's bravery inspired Da-Serin, the clan's Blade, to take Lu under her wing. Being sponsored by The Daj's Blade—the council's leader of the martial arts—resulted in Lu's fighting skills already being recognised as elite level.

The other positive from the tragedy was that the Daj, the clan's leader, had stepped down. Not that Daj-Veya had been a poor leader: quite the contrary. In her wisdom, she had proposed that in times of weather-driven crisis, the clan would be better served by a leader from the Wolf faction. At the annual Gathering, much to the Bear faction's ire, she had endorsed Da-Ula, whose acceptance by the clan began the current trend of integrationist activity.

Slowly at first, the Mobi'dern sent envoys, mercenaries, and martial arts teachers out into the world to obtain the money and goods required to replace their failing resources. Peace and prosperity had reigned since, though the Bears remained discontented.

The clan's cattle were relocated to eastern Yarrow, where lush valleys were irrigated from the Beck River. So began a new tradition of warrior candidates spending two moons in the North, at the farm's tannery. Once they had crafted their future uniform's raw materials, each candidate carried them home and dyed them Mobired using the pigments from the unique burnt umber coloured sand.

Dayla might lack the upper-body strength to secure her place in the clan, but her legs carried her at a pace that tested even Lu's endurance. Lu, determined not to fall behind, recalled Serin's words: *Distance is endured by the mind, not muscle.* As they entered the fourth bell of the run, she gritted her teeth, determined to best her companions. She noted how each girl ahead of her showed their weariness in different ways and made sure such signs did not betray her to Relik, who ran close on her heels.

They had been running across open fields that scaled the west side of Mount Arron, and after two bells neared a pass. Once through, they would begin the long descent into Raile. A road had come into view, arrowing towards the pass. They would follow it for a short time before parting with it on the other side of the peak.

Dayla leapt over a low, stone wall and turned onto the rutted track as they reached the pass, then halted abruptly, raising a fisted hand above her head. Each girl veered, fanning out, then froze in a defensive crouch, hands on their swords. Relik stopped beside Dayla and signed for an explanation for the pause. Before the young warrior could answer, Relik's head tilted and turned as she sensed the threat for herself.

Lu could also hear it. Metal rang on metal, and the frantic whickering of horses echoed off the pass's stone walls.

Lead us! Relik signaled to Nytis, ensuring the others saw her instruction. Lu felt a pang of jealousy. It was not unusual for a teacher to trust a warrior candidate, but she wished she had been given the opportunity to show her own mettle.

I'm the stronger warrior, she thought.

Nytis nodded and removed her bundle, signalling for the others to follow suit. Once the precious leather was stored behind a rock, the young woman assigned each a path forward: Relik to climb up the left side of the path, Lu to ascend the right. Nytis would advance up the centre of the pass with Dayla on her right side, with Jorak guarding her rear.

A sound formation, thought Lu, begrudgingly. She wished she had her prida; the eagle she dreamed about would circle above, feeding her information to confirm if the tactics were true. Lu reasoned Relik's Falli flew low and so had not detected the trouble ahead. Another mark against the species.

The group sprinted forward without a sound. Lu scaled the right side of the pass just high enough to gain a tactical advantage, but not so high she could not easily sweep down to support the unit. She glanced across and noted Relik did the same.

The road twisted in such a way that the ambush scene came into Lu's sight first; she halted and crouched. Instantly, the other women followed suit, waiting for her report.

A convoy of three wagons had been attacked. One lay on its side, having struck a rock in an attempt to flee. The horse that pulled it was injured. There were four dead men, three on the ground, and one on the wagon's bench. Two men, four women, and two girls had been rounded up as prisoners and were currently huddled by the third wagon, near the rear of the convoy.

Eighteen bandits surrounded the scene. Two appeared injured. On Relik's side, high up, was a man with a longbow; on Lu's side, two men with crossbows. All three had their backs to the Mobi'dern. They had positioned themselves to ambush the convoy, which had been heading west up the far side of the peak. Lu's hands flashed all of this information to Nytis as she took in the scene. She longed to add attack suggestions but knew it was not her place to do so.

A heartbeat later, Nytis's hands signalled her instructions. Jorak was to scale up to Lu's position, and once she arrived, Lu would lead the task of taking down the two crossbowmen. When they moved forward, Relik would attack the lone archer. She and Dayla would advance as closely as possible yet remain out of sight of the bandits. Once the long-range threats were neutralised, the group would descend on the outlaws-Relik on her own and the trainees in pairs. Lu and Jorak were to protect the prisoners, and the others would drive off or kill the bandits.

Lu flushed, her face tightening. She signalled that the two crossbowmen were close together and it would be easy for her to take them both; repeating the information she had sent initially. This was not her first blooding, and she felt confident in the task.

Nytis did not answer Lu but repeated her signal for Jorak to climb up to Lu's position. Lu scowled and said nothing. She glanced across at Relik who was focused on her own target, drawing a throwing knife, and readying her approach. Lu turned her attention to plan the best way for Jorak and her to conduct their attack. It was straightforward. A line of low scrub ran along the pass just above the crossbowmen, who had likely used it to hide from the convoy.

As Jorak reached her, Nytis gave Lu a moment to convey her plan before ordering the attack. Lu led, sensing the other girl close behind. They moved quickly behind cover, being careful not to dislodge a rock or startle birds and mountain-hares. It took Relik longer to move across exposed ground, pausing behind boulders until all three bowmen looked elsewhere.

Once their ambush was set, Nytis counted down from three on her fingers. As the last finger fell, so did the three bandits. Each had a bloody gash across his throat, through which his life gurgled out while his attacker caught his weight and lowered him down to the ground.

Lu wiped her knife on her victim and led Jorak down the steep rockface at a full sprint. Her eyes scanned the remaining bandits for long range weapons as they closed the distance. She made a beeline for the prisoners, drawing her sword as she reached over her head while running. She was six paces from the nearest man when a shout of alarm went up. As the bandit's head swivelled towards the sound, Lu cut it off his shoulders without breaking stride.

A few seconds later, Lu reached the prisoners and turned, dropping into Fifth Stance, a defensive posture. Jorak arrived a moment later and mirrored her, protecting the opposite flank. In that time, the other Mobi'dern had dispatched six bandits between them, and the others were turning to run. Nytis positioned her twosome between the fleeing men and the prisoners and gave the hand sign to halt the attack.

Chapter Three

Some warriors notch a strip of leather to track their kills; others write journals on pampa leaf, detailing their battles. The clan did not consider this prideful or trophy collecting; it is to respect the dead. Even if one hates the defeated or doesn't know them from Ag, one honours the moment when skill and fortitude, gathered in a life dedicated to the killing arts, take a soul. Lu did neither. She had no need. Each death was etched in her memory.

Her blooding had similarities to yesterday's skirmish with the bandits. She'd fought a cutthroat, a boy only two summers her senior. He was fast but untrained, and it lasted longer than it should have because she was reluctant to be brutal. It was not courage nor righteousness that delivered the killing blow; it was the fear of shame if she failed. Da-Serin had later confided that this was common for one's first kill.

Lu's second kill was a soldier, battle-trained and determined. It came when she was undertaking a skills test: to run alone from Dynos to Matalon—a step towards her Star Stone pin awarded for demonstrating independence. She pushed herself and arrived a full day early. She had to wait for her mentor, who was travelling separately, attending to other business.

Curious about town life, Lu waited on an inn's flat roof, watching the late-night townsfolk. Below, a drunken man cornered a serving girl by the woodshed, intent on forcing himself on her. He ignored Lu's shouts to stop, and when she approached, he attacked with malice. Despite the ale, his battle-hardened grit made it her toughest test. The vicious fight ended with her throwing knife piercing the large artery in his thigh as he raised his sword to cut her down.

All four men she had killed visited her dreams last night. Their complexion, posture, smell, and even her strikes were vivid, although she now realised, she had not seen the face of the crossbowman—only the back of his head. Yet her mind had preserved the image of every hair, the flakes of skin lodged in it, and the faded scar that resembled a crow's foot under his ear.

Relik had opted to escort the convoy to the next major town, assigning Dayla to lead the unit onward without her. Lu had no quarrel with Relik's choice—the woman was several years her senior—but Nytis's lack of faith during the battle still rankled. They would rendezvous with their teacher tomorrow morning at Smoot Lake, and Lu would seek to discuss the matter with her.

Why not offer Nytis some advice in the meantime?

Jorak led this leg of their journey at a relaxed pace, knowing they would reach the meeting point well ahead of Relik. Dayla ran second, then Lu, with Nytis as rearguard. Lu slowed and fell in step with her peer.

"No disrespect, but I would have handled matters differently at the ambush," Lu said. Nytis remained silent, but her expression encouraged Lu to speak her truth.

"The two crossbowmen were inattentive and relaxed. They had their backs to me. The bushes were thick, and the footing sound. Any of us could have taken them, but you didn't trust me. Keeping Jorak at your side offered better protective coverage for the prisoners."

"It wasn't a matter of lack of trust in you, Lu," Nytis replied, her eyebrows drawn together as she recalled events. "Had it been Relik on the side with two men, I would have given the same instruction. Had either man shouted out, the skirmish could have turned out very differently. I knew you would succeed, but I chose to ensure stealth until we were in the midst of the bandits."

Lu's mind evaluated Nytis's point objectively, replaying events from different perspectives. While it did so, she spoke without thinking.

"You should have trusted me more. I'm already considered elite at *the quiet death*."

"You get the irony in your words, don't you?" Dayla said, having slowed, curious about the discussion. Lu did not understand what she meant.

"You're upset you weren't trusted, but you are the most reluctant person I know when it comes to trusting others."

"That's not true," Lu said, flushing pink.

"When we are sparring in pairs, you extend your position to cover at least a third of your partner's space," Nytis said.

"I was responsible for checking our camp's perimeter last night, yet you followed soon after to reassure yourself that I hadn't missed anything," Jorak added from the front of the line.

Lu shook her head and unintentionally veered several feet away from the group. "That's not true, I . . ." But she knew it was.

The four candidates picked up the pace, re-established trail-discipline by settling back into their positions, leaving Lu to contemplate their words.

Chapter Four

Lu slid her rough leather pieces under the bunk in the hut she shared with F'Avati. The seasoned warrior was away in Nuulan, fulfilling the clan's pledge to protect the nation's leader, the Elect. Each season, four to six warriors took on this important, if somewhat dull, duty. Lu appreciated the space F'Avati's absence gave her, especially since the feedback from the others still troubled her.

As she often did when she needed to think, Lu decided to visit the wildlings. She would bathe later–the animals would not object to the smell of her long journey.

Her tree-hut was perched high in one of the massive Mobi trees near the centre of the village. Although Da-Serin was her mother-friend–the official sponsor to an orphan–Lu did not have sufficient status to share her tree. Instead, she lived in one adjacent. As she stepped out onto a four-stride-wide branch, she glanced across to see if the Blade was home. If so, she would pay her respects first, but there was no sign of the clan's lead warrior. Only Graff, the Blade's leopard, was visible, sprawling on the hut roof.

If Da-Serin had a canine or a breed of cat that preferred a lair, she would live in the caves below, among the cracks and fissures that ran through the region. Warriors typically lived where their prida felt most comfortable. Had that been the case, Lu would have been raised underground as well. She was grateful to live up high, where the avian prida constantly soared.

At the tree's base, Lu passed by the large communal buildings, most used for whatever duty was required. Only the Dajmut—the clan leader's meeting place—and the forges and kitchens had permanent roles. There was a light breeze on her face as she strode among the massive Mobi trunks, nodding greetings to those she passed. This route always gave her both a sense of peace and a small thrill in her belly as she approached the Wildlings' Hollow.

Lu stopped at the fence surrounding the shallow bowl where old mining tunnels had caused the ground to sink over hundreds of years. Only the roots of two massive trees prevented the earth from collapsing entirely. The Hollow's gate was open; she had never seen it closed in her lifetime–the future prida were too well trained to wander. An innate superstition made her pat the thick gatepost and say a small prayer that one day she would be accepted by a large bird of prey. Then her journey to warriorhood would be complete.

Only then could she set her sights on training to earn one of the clan's leadership positions.

The bitter politics of Bear versus Wolf were rooted in competing views on isolationism and had been responsible for her mother's death, and had also shaped Lu's lonely childhood. But the divide didn't stop at the question of how integrated the clan should be with the outside world. Like a creeping fungus, it infected every part of clan life, with each faction distorting unrelated matters to defend their core beliefs. Even decisions regarding daily routines or food supplies were bent to fit the agenda.

Lu, however, envisioned changes that would sweep away such attitudes, achieving the right balance at the right time—free from the toxic backdrop. Although she couldn't yet fully grasp the complexity of these entrenched conflicts, her confidence, tinged with the idealism of youth, made her fiercely determined to one day lead the clan and set things straight.

Da-Mirin was surprisingly young to hold the position of Lore on the Council of Old Women, having seen only forty-seven summers. The short, stocky woman kept her silver-white hair cropped shorter than her fingernails. When she glanced up, her piercing blue eyes skewered Lu, instantly ending the game she liked to play. Every candidate warrior tried to sneak as close as possible without detection; rumour had it that surprising Mirin in her own domain earned you the pick of the animals when the time came. Although Lore was not bonded with any of the prida-to-be, she was so in tune with them, she might as well have been. Everyone believed it was the animals alerting her to others' stealthy approaches that enabled her to enjoy her one hundred percent record of being unsurprised.

"Welcome home," was all she said before turning back to remove the porcupine quill from the paw of the young female mountain cat at her feet. The cat's tail flicked, but she did not deign to growl from discomfort as the Lore plucked out the sharp spine.

"Go now, cat," Lore said, pushing the cat away. The feline rolled to her feet, stepped close to Lu, and sniffed. Lu patted the cat's head as she looked up into the branches for Mowry, the largest eagle the Hollow had seen in years. He sat high up, next to another bird of prey half his size. The cat noticed one of the dogs had its head stuck down a burrow and trotted off to investigate.

"Here to watch the birds, young one?"

"That, and to think," Lu replied. "Do you think I lack trust?"

"Someone told you, at last?" In addition to her responsibility for all prida-candidates, the Lore's role was to know, and have final say on all clan history and tradition. This gave her an all-knowing air that extended to all matters, particularly those concerning warrior candidates. It was whispered that while the animal chooses the warrior, Lore held some subtle sway over the process. "Was it Nytis, or Jorak?"

"Both. And Dayla." Lu's mouth twitched into a smile, but her eyes flicked down to the ground as she slipped her hands into the folds of her tunic. "It wounds because they're right."

"For all your blind spots, young one, you're at least able to be objective. I'll give you that. Why do you think you find it so hard to trust?"

Lu had thought about little else since the others pointed it out, but just shrugged. *How can I increase my fighting skills to compensate?* She glanced up at the treetops. Da-Mirin followed her gaze.

"Why seek an eagle as your prida?" Da-Mirin asked. The sudden change of topic pulled Lu away from ruminating on trust, and she caught herself scowling–doing so in front of a council member could earn her latrine duties, so she quickly adjusted her expression and focused on the question.

"Not to be prideful, but I'm sure of my skills with a sword. And no disrespect to Relik, but her owl didn't give us any advance warning of some bandits we encountered on the way back from the cattle ranch. An eagle would be my eyes from above and has talons should I get into difficulties. It can dive in and wreak havoc, allowing me to regroup. It seems the best combination." She looked down and grinned. "And they are so pretty."

"Yet when that cat you just patted grows, and judging by her big, clumsy paws, she'll be huge, you'd have a fearsome fighting partner if she chose you."

"That's true, Lore. But it feels wrong for me."

"Your mother had a goshawk, you know. Best eyes I've ever seen," Da-Mirin said. Lu kept her head tilted down but wrenched her eyes up to meet Lore's. The older woman's gaze was unflinching. Lu met it but crossed her arms as if cold.

"The hawk flew low, his warning late."

"Then what do you think would have made a difference?" Da-Mirin asked.

"That the clan had cooperated with nearby settlements and were more diligent in guarding their crops. I understand they had to take turns to vote, but why did almost all go to vote at once? Why did Sofi and the others take so long to come to our aid?" Lu stopped, realising she had raised her voice. She hung her head. "I mean no disrespect."

"No disrespect to me? Or your mother? Or Sofi, or the clan?" Lore's voice was sharp enough to cause Lu to take a step back.

"To none of you. I'm sorry." Lu nearly jumped out of her skin when the large cat Lore had treated earlier nudged her hand. Da-Mirin laughed.

"Don't beat yourself up, young one. I was merely pointing out that your trust issues go back a long way. Even this oaf of a cat can sense your distress." The cat flopped down on her side and let out a long rumble of annoyance at Lore, then passed wind loudly. "Don't waste your wits worrying about what the girls said on the run. Think about Tekira and why you are still so angry at her."

"This dumb cat was just wiping the remains of the mererat she just ate on my hand to save herself the bother of grooming; it stinks. But I thank you for your wisdom and will think on what you've said. Is there anything I can help with today?"

After Da-Mirin sent Lu away to complete chores, she sat next to the cat and contemplated what she had observed.

"Well, this is going to be interesting," she whispered to the young mountain lion while stroking her side. She looked down to share a moment of anticipation, but the cat was already asleep.

Chapter Five

Annoyed that she did not feel the joy she expected, Lu shook her head, trying to clear her distracted thoughts. She tied off the wax-treated thread attaching her shoulder-buckle to her leather collar. This last stitch marked a seminal moment in the construction of the armour she would wear over her warrior clothing. Piece by piece she had dyed, shaped, and hardened each section over the past two moons. After many adjustments it fit her perfectly, and the buckles and straps could be let out as she grew.

The outfit and armour, which fit over it like an external skeleton, would not last forever. It could be damaged in battle or might need to be altered if her fighting style evolved. But a warrior's first set of leathers would be treasured for many years, no matter what came after. Yet instead of savouring this moment she had dreamt of since childhood, she felt unsettled.

Strange dreams plagued her sleep. Over her own musky scent, she caught whiffs of sour, pungent odours, despite how often she bathed. She knew these bodily changes were part of growing up-natural, but still embarrassing. F'Avati had returned several days earlier and had not mentioned it. Eventually, Lu asked if she was giving offense. The woman claimed not to smell anything odd, but with a conspiratorial grin complained that the grunting sounds Lu made in her sleep were keeping her awake. Lu's sleep had been fitful as she worried she would embarrass herself.

As if the changes in her body were not enough, she had taken to heart the advice that she must be more trusting of others. Hard to do when few warrior candidates matched her ability. To reach elite level quickly, every aspect of her behaviour had to be impeccable. Trusting less skilled candidates felt as if she were fighting her own nature.

She must win every sparring match—possible if singlehanded, but sparring paired with others in the traditional way left her vulnerable to her partners' shortcomings. And today would be such a test; she was paired with Dayla—who was far from the best swordswoman—against K'Tang, who would fight them single-handedly.

The two-on-one match was K'Tang's test of proficiency. The Blade and Daj-Ula, the clan's leader, would be observing. Lu's own performance would not "officially" count towards her own trials, but she had no doubt she would be judged by the Mobi'dern's top two warriors. Somehow, she had to trust Dayla as her partner while being prepared to compensate for any shortcomings.

Although a warrior candidate could not wear the clan's formal clothing until they advanced, they could wear their leather over-armour to spar. Despite her misgivings, Lu felt proud as she adjusted the buckles and clips, pleased that today's alteration placed the weight of her scabbard perfectly over her left shoulder blade. She checked everything one last time, then made her way down her tree and over to the training circles.

The spaces the clan used to train looked little like the nation's dojos or arenas where non-clan soldiers learn their trade. Each matt'e, as they were known, had flat central areas of varying sizes, and was surrounded by platforms, holes, trees, obstacles, and traps the trainers had concocted over hundreds of years. They were exposed to the elements, and prida of any kind could use the matt'e's features to their advantage.

The training ground was adjacent to the Wildlings' Hollow, and the matt'e K'Tang would face her test in butted up to the Hollow's fence. As Lu approach she noted Lore perched on a branch, three body lengths above the ground with a great view of proceedings. On her lap sat a pair of caracal kittens, one of which was pawing at a wolf cub beside the woman. Mowry preened two branches higher, while the young mountain cat stalked back and forth nervously a branch below.

That stupid cat looks more nervous than I feel, Lu thought. Ula's wolf sat panting in the shade of the fence, and Graff sat at Da-Serin's feet, his head up and alert as he sniffed the air. A formidable audience, but Lu felt a thrill in her body at the challenge.

K'Tang stood alone as Lu approached the matt'e. She was so still it was as if she was part of the tree at her back. As Lu crossed the circle's threshold, she stepped forward, and the two novices exchanged the traditional salutation in sign; *You move with the warrior's grace.*

Dayla came running up, late and slightly out of breath. They had until the Blade called them to fight to confer on tactics. Lu led Dayla out of earshot placing herself between the woman and K'Tang to prevent their opponent from reading their lips.

"You are senior," Lu said. "What is our plan?"

"Can we drop the pretence? We both know battle is where you excel, Lu. This is my last year to attempt the trials. I can't fail today, and I know you won't. What would you propose?" Lu admired the older woman's honesty, but her display of vulnerability made her uncomfortable. She fought to bury any negative feeling before they showed on her face and turned her mind to tactics.

"K'Tang is better than me, but with two of us, we can contain her. Her technique is faultless, and her strength and stamina make her relentless. She will seize on any slip, but she isn't creative, so she isn't likely catch us off guard and force mistakes." Dayla nodded her understanding, so Lu continued.

"If K'Tang were weaker, and if you were stronger, with all due respect, I would choose offence. We would split so one of us could work around and attack her flank, if not her back." Lu paused, thinking things through. "Today we will stay together and keep the fight on the ground. If she climbs the terrain, we lose manoeuvrability and cohesion, and she gains the advantage, so instead, we'll fall back and wait for her to come down. She must win today; we can afford to wait her out.

"We'll favour basic and mid-level stances and techniques; mount a solid, if boring, defence. Protect our own quarters and, by doing so, protect each other. We break formation only if the other is compromised. Agreed?"

Dayla nodded and let out a long breath. Lu suspected she had worried Lu would have wanted to be more aggressive. *Patience today, but when my turn comes to be the solo warrior, I'll show them what real aggression looks like.*

"Prepare!" Blade said, not raising her voice but heard by everyone within fifty strides.

The three combatants approached the armourer's table and were handed various cuttletis. Each band was sized to buckle around a wrist, thigh, neck, or other vulnerable point on the body. Slivers of wood, half a finger's length, protruded around the band to hold a thin strip of leather thong away from the skin. If the slivers or thong are cut by a sword stroke, then that part of the body is deemed struck. The referee calls out if the damage is fatal or the extent of the damage, and the fighters must act as if the injuries were real.

"Positions!" called Culla, the referee for this bout.

The instruction "positions" referred to taking First Stance, not any specific location within the matt'e. K'Tang moved quickly to the circle's centre, drew her blade from her back, and struck the traditional pose. Lu led Dayla across the space to the far side and turned so they had a wall two strides behind them, protecting their back. That location also forced K'Tang to swivel to face them. Not only did this undermine the power move that K'Tang had pulled, but it also meant she had the Blade and Daj behind her, which Lu hoped would make her feel disrespectful or unsettled.

Dayla withdrew her blade, and Lu delayed several breaths, pretending to look around, taking in the spectacle. If it had any effect on K'Tang, she did not show it. The woman looked completely relaxed and focused. Lu did notice Lore smile and felt a heartbeat of petty triumph until she realised she was distracting herself. She pulled her sword and lowered herself into the stance. A second later, Culla signalled the start, and K'Tang launched forward in a blindingly fast flurry of strokes.

Lu thought K'Tang would first target Dayla, their weak point, but she was mistaken. The initial ferocious burst came directly at her– high, low, high, low–each strike separated by K'Tang inching closer. Lu countered the advance by giving ground, relieved that Dayla was also falling back and not tempted to hold in her initial location. Staying put as K'Tang advanced past her would give Dayla access to her opponent's flank but it would have split their defence in the first seconds of the bout.

With the wall behind them looming, Lu gave the signal to pivot right. Dayla slowed her retreat as Lu rotated around her, putting the wall at her right side. Once they had turned ninety degrees, they matched each other's steps, retreating in unison under K'Tang's onslaught.

She is relentless, but we can maintain this far longer than her. As this thought occurred K'Tang changed tactics. She delivered three lightning-fast slashes at Dayla's front foot, positioned right on the border between Lu and Dayla's zones, before spinning back and to her left, out of reach of Lu's blade.

That was a test to see if I would cross zones to cover for Dayla. A past failing of mine, my friend. Lu smiled inwardly, pleased that she had not reacted, and that Dayla had not been flustered, neatly fending K'Tang off.

K'Tang kept her momentum, putting some distance between them. She did not turn to face her foe, instead she picked up speed before leaping onto a raised platform, then onto a wide beam that would put her above Dayla's shoulder if she ran along it.

"Centre," Lu said, her voice calm, and Dayla followed her back to K'Tang's starting point, away from the threat.

Lu saw K'Tang glance over at the clan's leaders. *She recognises we are well organised and patient and she is worried.* K'Tang ran two steps along the beam before somersaulting off. As she twisted in the air, she slid her sword back into its scabbard, landing in a full sprint towards Dayla. As she neared, she feinted pulling her throwing knives, tricking Dayla into stepping back and raising her blade. Lu registered the attacker's weight shift forward. *She's going low!* K'Tang ducked into a shoulder roll and emerged feet first, kicking Dayla in the left rib and knocking her onto her back.

"Broken ribs," Culla said. Lu kept one eye on K'Tang as she rolled away instead of following up on her advantage. She glanced at her partner's cuttletis. The left-side one hung by its thong, shattered. As Dayla snapped back to her feet, Lu could see the cuttletis on her back was also damaged. Lu agreed with the referee's assessment that such damage from the fall was unlikely to cause harm to a Mobi'dern.

Lu and Dayla regrouped in their defensive position, but Dayla would need to keep her left arm down, close to her side to honour the simulated injury. K'Tang had run to the weapons rack on the far wall and turned back to them holding two long spears, one in each hand.

I take it back, she can be creative. Perplexed at this unconventional attack, Lu gave the hand sign for Dayla to drop back a pace and cover her left rear quarter. With Dayla's injury, it was now appropriate for Lu to take a more aggressive lead rather than fight as equal partners. She led Dayla to the right and backed up until they reached a thick, vertical post that supported an overhead platform. She positioned them so the post was on Dayla's left, providing a thin barrier to an attack of the girl's weakened flank.

K'Tang had not stood idle while Lu reorganised. After twirling each spear around her to sense their weight and balance, she began to sprint toward her combatants. Lu took a step away from the wall and adopted Eighth Stance, ideal for fending off long weapons. K'Tang leapt, and mid-flight threw first one, then the other spear, reaching back over her shoulder for her blade as she landed. Lu assessed the trajectory of the spears; they would pass harmlessly between herself and Dayla; *no threat.*

Yet as her mind processed the situation, Lu knew something was off. K'Tang was the best candidate in a decade. There were whispers she would replace Da-Serin as Blade one day, which angered the older candidates who sought the position. Lu wanted to contend for it too. K'Tang would not waste one spear, let alone two.

As K'Tang's blade came free and she shifted her path towards Dayla, Lu grasped the nature of the attack. The two spears had lodged in the wall behind her, and their shafts formed a barrier between herself and her partner. With the post added in, K'Tang had isolated the injured Dayla for the moments it would take Lu to either chop through the spears or step around them. Her training resolved the timing and angles in her mind, and she knew K'Tang would be on Dayla several rapid heartbeats before Lu could make her way past the impromptu obstacle.

K'Tang's blade arm whipped up into a high strike position, while her other arm dropped back for balance. Dayla turned to her left, bringing her good arm up and raising her sword to defend against the attack.

As Lu watched K'Tang rise to deliver her downward strike, an image–like an unbidden memory or forgotten instinct–flashed into her mind. She had no time to process it and acted on reflex. She slammed her lead foot down, halting her momentum, and thrust her blade between the spears blocking the path to her partner's defence.

K'Tang's balancing arm whipped forward, and a concealed throwing knife that Lu had somehow spotted flew at Dayla's thigh. It would have severed the cuttletis representing the girl's main artery had the tip of Lu's blade not deflected it. The knife still grazed Dayla's calf, which was better than the alternative.

"Halt!" Culla shouted, bringing the bout to an immediate end. Minor injuries in bouts between full warriors were permitted, but not in those with candidates.

"I'm sorry," Lu said, stepping over the lowest spear. K'Tang was already at Dayla's side, checking the injury.

"It's just a love bite," she said, using the term warriors used for nicks and grazes.

"I'll name that one after you, Lu," Dayla said with a laugh. K'Tang helped Dayla to her feet and the three combatants walked to the centre of the matt'e, breathing hard and sweating profusely, then stood at attention.

"Draw!" Culla said, repeating the score in hand sign. "Lu deflected the killing strike, but K'Tang's follow-through would have put Dayla out of the fight. Lu was not in position for an immediate counterstrike, which would have turned the match into one-on-one combat. With neither Lu nor K'Tang injured, we cannot anticipate the outcome."

All four women bowed to each other, and the crowd relaxed. Some came forward to talk through the events while others dispersed. The crowd parted as Da-Serin approached and gave each participant a clap on their shoulder. She did not look at Dayla's scratch, since doing so would embarrass a candidate.

Lu glanced over at Lore, noticing that she had moved during the bout. Now, she sat a branch lower, stroking the mountain lion, who had become quite agitated.

"Walk with me," Da-Serin said to Lu. When they were out of earshot, she continued. "I just wanted to share that both Daj-Ula and I were impressed by what you did back there. Well done."

"Thank you, but I think K'Tang would have bested me had the bout continued. My interception of the knife was clumsy, and without the cuttletis, she would have thrown it two inches farther from me and struck the artery. I wouldn't have reached it."

"I don't mean the knife. Neither of us even saw it. K'Tang hid it brilliantly. How you spotted it, I can't imagine. No, we were impressed with how you led Dayla. She clearly trusted you, and despite her injuries she acquitted herself well enough. We just agreed to recommend she be raised to warrior. She may never be the best fighter, but she's survived enough trials. You helped her be good enough."

"I don't understand," Lu replied, shaking her head.

"She's always tried to compensate for her lack of physical strength by being overaggressive. Since you've taken her under your wing, she's learned to accept a support role. A team player."

"But I haven't taken her under my wing." The Blade roared with laughter at Lu's honesty, and put a hand on her shoulder, halting their walk.

"Yet she trusts the leader in you, Lu," Blade replied, leaning in. "You are still too focused on your own path, but others sense the change. The best version of you is beginning to emerge. Don't grasp for her; let her come to you. But trust my words, Lu, you can grow into council material given time."

Chapter Six

Lu returned her sparring equipment to her hut. She was so buoyed by the success of the fight that she felt like she was floating as she made her way back down to the ground, her steps light and full of energy. Others added to her sponsor's praise to the extent that Lu retreated into the hills to escape the attention. Once she had run off some energy, she had sought out K'Tang. The girl hid her disappointment behind her typical gruff stoicism but warmed when she realised Lu had not come to gloat.

Lu had carefully chosen her words to avoid offence, but she was curious about why K'Tang had radically changed her tactics for this bout. It was clear that she had developed a plan beforehand, and the creativity and risk involved were a departure from the norm for the cohort's lead fighter. K'Tang admitted she sought a quick win to impress the Daj, to create distance between herself and Lu, whom she saw as her nearest competitor.

This backhanded praise from K'Tang lingered in her mind as she settled into her bunk, accompanying the many versions of the bout that replayed in Lu's mind as she fell asleep.

Her dreams were disturbing as the bout repeated over and over, each retelling showing just a piece of the match. Some mirrored what she had experienced, but many were different.

In two, the bout did not start; she arrived late in one, and in the other, she arrived without her sword. In a third, K'Tang was late, but they allowed the start, and Lu beat her in the first few seconds. In another, the first spear K'Tang threw lodged in Lu's thigh. In another, Daj-Ula was referee, insisting all weapons be left outside the matt'e and the combatants only grapple and kick.

As odd as these dreams were, they were not what truly unsettled Lu. Even in sleep, she knew her mind was processing fears and ideas, and they felt familiar. Yet some scenes felt foreign, as if viewed from a distance and from above. Part of what made them odd was that if Lu had actually viewed a bout from that perspective, the distance of the scene would have made things blurry. Yet the images were as sharp in detail as she experienced up close. *No one could have such sharp vision.*

If clarity had been the only odd aspect of the distant segments, it would not have been so bad, but the images seemed to compete with each other. Unlike the scenes viewed up close, these segments were rife with emotion. Each distant scene was a moment in the match with Lu under extreme pressure: the initial tirade of strikes, when Lu worried Dayla would not pivot, and the relief when she did; the moment Lu realised the advantage K'Tang gained with her spear tactic; and the last, most instinctive but desperate lunge to intercept the knife.

This last scene repeated perhaps a dozen times, each version vying for dominance like two young siblings fighting over something they both coveted. Both strident and needy, the win all-important, yet with the sense one sibling did not truly care and fought only because the other desperately wanted the prize. The intensity of the struggle woke her. She grasped at the last few vivid repeats until they faded like wisps of smoke. All she retained was a sense that the viewpoints were from a similar direction but different heights. In some she could see the throwing knife in K'Tang's hand, while in others, it was hidden.

Lu's sleep was not disturbed for long. Pride and relief soon replaced worry and curiosity and if she dreamt again, she could not recall. She woke feeling fresh, energised, and as if she were a few inches taller. A warmth she enjoyed until she reached the Dajmut for the routine interview with the Council of Old Women, and it was brutally ripped away.

In the year before a candidate was expected to take the trials of warriorship, the council reviewed their progress every other moon. Each novice attended six meetings in total and listened in silence as their sponsor gave a stark, factual accounting of both their highs and lows. No one sat at council meetings; the leaders gathered casually in a rough circle, while others required to participate positioned themselves around the walls. Candidates remained at attention throughout in the circle's centre, feeling vulnerable.

As was typical, the positives were listed first. Da-Serin dispassionately presented a long list of accomplishments, including the signs of teamwork and leadership improvement evidenced by Dayla's recent growth. The list of negatives began with things Lu considered benign—but they stung nonetheless—such as inattention here, or a missed detail there. All candidates were held to such high standards and such feedback was common. But then the tone in the room chilled.

"Relik, please step forward and give your account," Blade said. The warrior who had fought beside Lu at the ambush stepped forward and concisely described the lead up to the skirmish, focusing on Lu's part in it.

"To summarise, Lu's actions made it clear she resented Nytis's leadership. Her interruption of the planning, inserting unnecessary opinions and options, confirmed it. Had I been in Nytis's place I might have left the two bowmen to Lu—she's skilled enough—but either plan was solid. Lu arguing in the moment was the biggest threat to our success. Had Nytis been less sure of herself, things might have devolved."

Lu felt sick. This was harsh criticism, made worse by the painful truth of it, her flaws laid bare before those she respected most.

"But that's not what worries me most," Relik said. Lu tensed. *What more could there be?*

"I escorted the survivors to Bearton and had my owl monitor the unit's progress. Through her, I eavesdropped on part of a discussion that makes it clear not only had Lu exhibited trust issues—we knew that, of course—but all of the girls knew and even made light of it." Lu felt the urge to defend herself. She'd taken their feedback and made the effort to change, hadn't she? She clamped her teeth together and stared at the floor, her cheeks on fire.

"In their naivety, the girls adapted and joked about it. In fairness to Lu, I've observed her attempting to correct the fault. I'd even venture that her efforts contributed to Dayla's progress. But such issues are rooted in character, which is as difficult to change as reputation."

"Lu has all of her pins and will score well in the trials, I'm sure," Blade said, taking over the conversation. From the corner of her eye Lu saw Relik retreat to her space by the wall. "Even if she is unable to build on recent progress, she will ascend to warrior status, perhaps with a score lower than she would like. But the bigger question is: will a prida choose her? We all know they are sensitive to negative emotions within the group, and they are easily put off." Lu's world lurched.

Are they going to make me skip a year?

"Lore, your thoughts?" Lu's eyes inappropriately shot up to the woman. She forced them back to the floor.

"When Lu comes to the Hollow, the animals react strongly to her. She definitely has their attention. But their behaviour is off; she causes competition and contention, rather than curiosity and desire." Lu winced as Lore addressed her directly. "Your hut-mate reports that you sleep poorly. How are your dreams, girl?"

Lu felt betrayed. F'Avati was not a close friend, but still . . .

"My dreams have been strange of late," Lu replied. "I've been putting more effort into training, so I'm more tired. Though I am fresh in the mornings. I don't believe the dreams are impacting my performance—"

"I wouldn't advise pulling her from this year's contest," Lore said, cutting Lu off. The sudden wave of relief made it seem as though Lore spoke with a slight chuckle, but if there was any humour, the Daj quickly extinguished it.

"Well, Da-Serin. It would be embarrassing if the Blade's charge didn't get a prida. It's two moons to the trial, and she must bond within a moon or two afterward. Work it out. Next candidate."

Da-Serin gave a sharp flick of her fingers, signalling for Lu to leave. She stumbled from the Dajmut while fighting desperately to keep her emotions from her face, terrified others might see her fear.

Mobi'dern don't fear, my little warrior, her mother's voice echoed from the past. Tears boiled into her eyes as she ran, though she could not tell if it was from shame or heartbreak.

*

Once the Council of Old Women's business concluded for the day, Daj-Ula asked the Blade and Lore to stay as the others filed out. Her aide brought in fresh lemon tea before they retreated to the hut's seating area. Once they were settled, the Daj spoke.

"Well, Serin, you and Relik certainly scared young Lu. If she doesn't get the message today, she never will."

"To be honest, I think she's most of the way there already. Today was just reinforcement of the message."

"She all but ran out of the hut. I hoped she believed the lie about Relik hearing the gossip through her owl. Jorek will suffer if it's revealed that she was the one who brought the concern to you."

"Jorek's a wise one," said Da-Serin. "She has only Lu's best interests at heart. She'll rise through our ranks, I'm sure."

"What will you do with Lu between now and the trials?" Lore asked.

"I was going to ask for your counsel. Should she be spending more time with the animals? If not, I'll assign her a task away from Mobi for a few weeks to help her settle."

"I'm curious, too," Daj-Ula said, looking at her Lore. "I heard what you told Lu, but where do you think she stands? Will she earn a prida?"

"They were fighting over her, that's clear enough," the woman replied with an enigmatic smile. "She's a girl of rare ability. One is likely to choose her. The real issue is, how will Lu react if it's not the one she covets?"

"Is there something we can do to influence Mowry?" Da-Serin asked. The Lore set her cup down, stood, and walked to the hut's entrance. She paused, glancing over her shoulder with an unreadable expression.

"Oh, I think it's too late for all that," was all she said before wandering out, leaving the other two women in confusion.

Chapter Seven

Lu knew her sponsor as two distinctly different people. Most of the time she was the Daj's Blade–unbending, ruthless, fair, precise–but occasionally she was Da-Serin. This softer version was not maternal, but had humour, compassion, and occasional flashes of affection. She was glad it was the former who summoned her to brief her on her mission; standing in front of the latter would have made Lu's shame untenable.

The Blade was all business. Veya, the clan's former Daj, needed to journey to Dynos, the region's capital. She wished to travel incognito and make some stops along the way, with Lu posing as her daughter. With Veya having seen nearly seventy summers, they would ride rather than travel on foot. It would have been insulting to suggest Veya needed protection or assistance, so the specifics of Lu's role were not discussed.

All Mobi'dern learn to ride, but with the clan's focus on endurance and fitness, it felt like cheating. Veya made it clear from the outset she hated how her age made her reliant, and she was unapologetic about being cranky because of it. She was at their rendezvous point early; her pony perfectly saddled. She clucked and pecked at Lu's effort to prepare her own mount, commenting and correcting every step. Disguised as villagers, they trotted out under a cloud of annoyance.

Four bells into the ride, the desert gave way to mountains, and they stopped for a meal. Twice, Veya called Lu by her daughter's name, "Lika," without realising it. Lu did not think too much of it until the woman began to disrobe.

Has she lost her mind? Lu realised that 'accompanying' the ex-Daj meant compensating for her mental lapses. This thought was reinforced when the old woman, dressed only in loose undergarments, turned and her scrawny legs carried her off the main trail into the foothills. Her gait retained the hallmark Mobi lope of endurance, though at a pace Lu could match at a fast walk.

"Bring my pony!" Veya called over her shoulder.

Lu quickly gathered Veya's discarded clothing, neatly folded it– she would give no excuse for another scolding–and took the reins of both horses. The old warrior had covered more distance than Lu expected by the time she caught up. Veya was sweating hard, but her breath was calm and even.

"Healer Merri won't let me run. Says my heart can't take the heat. But it's cooler here in the hills, and my old bones need this to stay strong."

"I don't think you should—"

"Did I ask you, girl?"

They ran in silence until they reached a tarn high in the hills. Veya had clearly been here before and directed Lu on where to go to find fresh water and firewood after she had seen to their mounts.

As she took care of her assigned chores, she kept half an eye on her charge. *It wouldn't surprise me if the crazy woman dived in the water next.* It would be freezing, and they were close enough to the south that the water would be dangerously contaminated with minerals washed down from the dry hills during storms.

When she got back to the campsite, Veya had laid out both of their bedrolls—an extravagance afforded by having horses—and was sound asleep. Lu lit the fire, banked it so it would last through the night, and lay down. She would not show weakness. She set her mind to wake instantly if Veya got up in the night—she might run off—and then closed her eyes.

Sleep did not come, but the darker thoughts Lu had held back through the day did. The silence, split by her companion's snoring, broke the walls Lu carefully maintained.

This woman led the clan when my mother was murdered.

How many times had Lu wondered: if the treatment of adjacent settlements had been kinder, would she still be an orphan? Why were there not more guards? Why did help not come quickly? Did this woman at her side ever lose sleep over these same thoughts? The loud, breathy buzzing of Veya's snoring answered that question on this night, at least.

How many times had Lu wished she had the courage to ask the ex-Daj these questions? Surrounded by the clan—a decade gone by now—Lu always had the excuse of propriety. One did not simply approach someone in Veya's position to talk, let alone to accuse, however well-disguised as curiosity. But here, alone on the trail? Now it would require a different kind of courage, one Lu was not sure she could summon. Though bravery was usually her strong suit, she feared it might desert her once again by morning.

*

Several days into the ride, Lu almost wished she was back in Mobi facing her shame. *At least there, I could practice teamwork and improve my flaws.* Veya's tongue was sharper than her blade. *If the council sought to punish me, they hit their mark.* She felt a pang of guilt at the thought; Veya's prida had passed the summer before, and the woman had refused a new one, citing her age. *Being without a bond-mate must be difficult.*

It should have taken seven days by horse to reach Dynos, but their journey took twice as long. Veya tarried with friends along the way, and on four occasions, she insisted on forsaking her horse and running. Lu felt they were the longest days of her life.

"We all prefer to run, Veya, but are you not concerned you will miss your appointments in Dynos?" Lu asked, her frustration giving her a voice.

"Nonsense, girl. Nothing wrong with horses. I had a warrior who bonded with one. Can you imagine? The things they achieved together."

The old woman claimed the appointments would wait and rebuked Lu for her lack of patience.

In Dynos, Lu got an unexpected reprieve. They stopped at an inn owned by a longstanding friend, a man a few years Veya's junior. Apparently, he and his brother had owned the business since their father had passed and boasted several generations of being the hub of the local community.

"This is one of our best candidates," Veya said by way of introduction. "She has her mother's patience, putting up with me on this journey." The unexpected praise and mention of her mother made Lu's throat tighten. "She looks like Tekira, too."

The man stepped a pace closer and studied Lu intently, making her uncomfortable.

"And now, as her reward," Veya said, throwing Lu a small leather purse, "she can go off on her own and explore Dynos, in all its glory and seediness."

"But the Blade assigned me the task of–"

"She's not here. You'd prefer to wait on me some more?" There was a glint of humour in the old woman's eyes that had not been present on the trail. Lu hesitated, unsure what to do.

"Return promptly in three mornings' time. My horse had better be perfectly saddled and loaded with supplies." The sharpness of the command spurred Lu into action, exactly as the old woman had intended.

"And don't forget to train! I promised Serin you'd be in top shape for the trials, and we will have to ride hard to get back in time."

Chapter Eight

Lu had no interest in exploring Dynos. She was not dressed as a Mobi'dern, and knew its streets concealed thugs and criminals who would not hesitate to rob or attack a woman alone. She had no qualms about killing such people, but worried that an entanglement with the authorities would make her miss the trials.

At night, she slept under the trees in the forests north of the city, with her blade wrapped in her bedroll, only taking it out to train hard each morning and evening. During the day, she ventured into town, hating the crowds but marvelling at the height of the buildings and the abundance in the many marketplaces. On the second day, she ran out to see Agspire. The headquarters of the Bredden Order was immense, the only structure she had ever seen taller than the old growth Mobi trees at the centre of her village.

After three days Lu travelled back to the inn. She arrived at seventh bell with supplies in hand for the trip home and circled to the rear of the two-story structure and entered the stables. The man who led her to the ponies' stall so closely resembled the owner Lu knew instantly he must be the brother. And there was something else familiar about him but she could not imagine where they might have met.

"I cleaned all your tack," he said, pointing to their ponies' saddles and leatherwork neatly laid out on a bench. "Can I help you dress them?" His voice was warm, yet a little too friendly. Something in the question set Lu on edge. A heartbeat later, she realised it was his phraseology. "Dress them," was a term favoured by the clan. Others would say, "tack up," or "saddle," or something similar. Although they were supposed to be incognito, Veya had not hidden their clan affiliation from the innkeeper.

"You know our ways," Lu said. She took charge of Veya's horse and accepted his help with her own. If hers was not perfect, Veya might not notice. Of course, Lu would check it later.

They worked in silence, and soon the ponies were ready, with the supplies tucked into various saddlebags. Throughout, Lu had sensed the man watching her. It was not leery or intrusive. Most outsiders are either awed by or afraid of the clan, so it was not unusual to be stared at.

"You look like her, you know," said the man. Lu tilted her head, eyebrows furrowing as she pulled down on the girth strap, trying to decipher his statement. Then he added, "Tekira."

Lu's heart skipped a beat as her head snapped around, and she stepped out from behind Veya's pony.

"You knew my mother?"

"Yes. She always stayed with us when she visited Dynos."

"What was she like?" Lu had heard about her mother from others—a skilled warrior and leader, with many martial accomplishments. Disciplined to a fault, wise, yes, but with a sense of fun that often led others to overlook her point.

"Warm. Compassionate. A deep thinker with a wicked sense of humour," the man replied. "I miss her still."

Lu was stunned. The woman the man described was far from the portrayal that others had given her. He must be confused, and she was about to say so.

"You resemble her but look a lot like me, too."

"I . . . I don't understand!" Lu's mind stopped functioning. Questions began to coalesce but evaporated before they fully formed. She just stared. Looking at him was like staring into still water and seeing a distorted reflection—a version of herself, but not quite right.

"Veya and your mother were great friends. They often travelled together, and we . . . well my brother and I . . . well you know why Veya stays here, right?" The man blushed, his hands rising defensively.

"You are an all-female clan. You know how babies are made, don't you?" His look of pride had turned to embarrassment, and now horror. Silence reigned and Lu could not decide if she wanted Veya to arrive and end the conversation or stay away. The pieces of the puzzle slowly slipped into place.

"You're my father?"

"I believe so. She told me we had a daughter, but she never brought you here. I asked Veya who you were when my brother said you looked like Tekira, but she would not answer. But now that I see you . . . you are clearly my daughter."

While her heart and mind swirled with questions and emotions, a cold anger settled like a stone in Lu's stomach.

"Why wouldn't Veya have told me?"

"Well, she loved your mother like a daughter. Her own daughter was . . . difficult. Your mother's death was hard for Veya. It's still raw, today."

"She's responsible for my mother's death!" The cold pit of anger flared into a bonfire of rage, and the words escaped before she could stop them.

"No. No . . ." the man stammered. "That's not the case–"

"I don't know what tale she's told you, but she has blood on her hands."

"You're wrong. Although Veya agrees with you–her guilt hasn't dwindled with time. She blames herself entirely. It's the stories from others who come here that shed a different light. Look, I didn't–"

Lu grabbed the reins of both ponies and pulled them out of the stalls and into the street. On some level, she knew it was the jolt of meeting her father she could not face. Resenting and blaming Veya was a familiar storm she could easily hide within.

Water splashed on Lu's wrist, and she feared the hot burning in her eyes was turning into humiliating tears. Relief washed over her when she realised it was in fact just a fat raindrop, quickly followed by its siblings. The heavens opened abruptly, and she welcomed the downpour–another storm to hide in.

Veya stepped out of the inn, holding the innkeeper's forearms warmly as she said her goodbyes. Lu raised her hood and glowered from beneath it as the rain pounded down. The old woman took one look at Lu, and her pace slowed. She glanced at the man in the stable doorway. His eyes were red, his expression pained. He shrugged an apology. Veya shook her head, but her face remained unreadable as she walked up to Lu and took the reins of her pony.

"Do you wish to wait out the storm in the stables, girl?" Veya's tone was harsh, but a brittleness undercut her words. Lu turned her back, swung up into her saddle, and tugged her cloak down over her thighs.

Veya took her time mounting and settling her own cloak, bracing herself to endure the storm ahead. Without a glance back at Lu or the two men, she kicked her pony into a canter and disappeared into the torrent. Lu looked at her father, etching his face into her memory before following the old woman. As she rode away into the rain, she realised with a pang of regret that she had not even asked his name.

Chapter Nine

In Mobi, work did not wait for the sunrise in the Wildings' Hollow. Those animals that ate at dawn or dusk were led to the hunting grounds to feed. If they caught nothing, food would not be offered; a prida that could not live off the land, did not track, and would not kill, was a pet, not a warrior's aid. As Lore stood in the Dajmut at the tenth bell, after two hours of boring meetings, she yearned for the days her duties were to run with the animals, not discuss logistics at council meetings.

At last, the final item was dealt with and the meeting broke.

"Take breakfast with me," Da-Ula said to her council of six. The Teacher was accountable for all clan knowledge that was not lore or martial in nature. Forge ensured the clan was armed and armoured, while the Will-Warden managed all commerce, trade, and activities with outsiders. The Hearth oversaw the clan's food and living logistics as well as the many women who did not achieve warrior status. All four had pressing duties and declined the invitation.

Blade and Lore sat after the Daj had taken her place. A simple meal was served, and the three enjoyed a pleasant respite from their relentless responsibilities. It was cut short when a teenage girl burst through the hut's door, her ragged breaths preventing her from explaining her panicked arrival. Lore recognised her from the Hollow's staff and stood to intercept her. Once the girl caught her breath, they conversed in whispers.

"You've done nothing wrong, Elli. Go back to the Hollow and wait for me. Get some breakfast and rest." When the girl left, Lore came back to the table, sat, and sipped her tea. Her eyes sparkled and the corners of her mouth twitched as she processed the news.

"You look like the cat who caught the mouse," the Blade said with a grin. "What did she do?"

"She nearly killed herself running from the hunting grounds. It's a shame Elli's not warrior material considering her bravery. She wanted to run in the other direction but came here anyway."

"What could she be so afraid of?" the Daj asked.

"One of the prida she was minding ran away. She expected to be punished for losing one of her charges."

"Which prida? What's happened? I've never heard of a prida running away." The Daj and her Blade sat up and leant closer.

"It was the mountain lion. I believe your plan is working, Serin." Lore said with an enigmatic smile.

"My plan? What plan?"

"You think Lu needs to confront the pain and anger she feels about her mother's death to make elite level. Sending her with Veya was not subtle." The Blade, looking less like the clan's fiercest warrior and more like a mischievous teenager, glanced at the Daj, but she still seemed puzzled.

"I admit it. I think Lu and Veya need to clear the air," Blade said.

"But what does the cat have to do with anything?" the Daj asked.

"Oh, she's sensed her bond-mate's distress and is running to her."

"Her bond-mate? But the cat is still an initiate, not a full prida. She can't be bonded yet."

"Lu's grunting at night? Strange dreams? She saw K'Tang's hidden knife through the cat's eyes, I suspect," Lore said.

"The cat's chosen Lu? Does the girl know?"

"Absolutely no clue. She only has eyes for Mowry, who ignores her all day, making Lu want him even more."

"But isn't it too early to bond? We haven't had the trials," Blade said.

"It happens rarely," Lore replied. "Only once before in my lifetime, but it's well documented in the scripts. Roughly once in a generation."

"Who was the last?" asked the Daj.

"Tekira," the Blade said, taking the name off Lore's lips, and deflating a little of her smugness.

Chapter Ten

Veya kept up an astonishing pace for two bells, riding her pony hard through the Dynos streets, across the Beck River, and onto the road south. She only eased up when the rain turned the track to mud and the pony was at risk of injury. A bell later, she paused to eat and relieve her bladder. Lu was glad of the break. A combination of rarely riding and the damp saddle was causing chafing. *If the old woman can tolerate it, I'll not complain.*

By nightfall, the torrent had reduced to a light drizzle, and they reached the Forest of Yarin. The thick old-growth canopy kept out both the moisture and the moonlight, so Veya declared it was time to camp. They dismounted, and the old woman sat staring off into the trees while Lu built a fire and hung out the wet items to dry.

Lu had fumed and brooded all day, and the wet conditions had only stoked her anger. They sat in moody silence, pecking at food from their supplies and staring at the flames until the wind picked up. A new storm front brought heavier rain that penetrated their leafy shelter. Lu used some leather cord from her pack to string up their travelling cloaks and create a shelter for each of them. It would keep them dry and protect the fire set between them from being extinguished by the downpour.

Sitting in the near dark under her cloak, listening to the rain simmer on the leaves above left Lu with nothing to do but ruminate on the anger that was bubbling within. Although the fire flickered, the conditions robbed it of its heat and most of its light. Lu sat cold, glaring into the darkness under Veya's cloak, the old woman only visible when lightning lit up the clearing. Both of Lu's inner thighs were sore, and the right one had blistered–a humiliation for a warrior. Adding salt to the wound, the old woman did not seem to be suffering from the insane pace she set.

Lu fidgeted and shifted, finding no comfort on the leafy forest floor and unable to dispel the storm raging within. Three times Lu opened her mouth to speak to Veya, only to clamp down on her lips when she realised only vitriol and spite shaped what she had been about to say.

"Say what's on your mind, girl," Veya said from the darkness on her side of the fire. "You've been sour all day, and you won't sleep unless you get it off your chest. I don't want to hear you huff and puff all day tomorrow, too."

Lu's rage spiked, but being confronted by the ex-Daj caught her off guard and choked her first retort. She did not speak for a while, partly because her mind whirled like the wind above and partly because there was a childish satisfaction in making the woman wait. She suddenly felt churlish and forced herself to speak.

"Why didn't you tell me that man was my father?" Though she intended to sound calm, the words strained through gritted teeth.

"Is that what you want to ask me, girl? The clan has only one use for a man, and you've spent more of your life fuming at me than thinking of him. Tomorrow, the storm will pass, and you won't have the lightning in you to confront me. Be a warrior, not a waster. You can visit him at any time, but you only get one shot at me."

The questions that festered in Lu's mind churned, each demanding to be asked first. Why the policies antagonising the settlements? Why did help not come? Why is Veya so revered and honoured for her wisdom at passing command to Ula, even after so many poor decisions?

"Why did you kill my mother?" was all that came out of her mouth. It was a cold voice, so quiet and devoid of emotion that it shocked Lu, and she raised her hand to her lips as if she could take back her words.

"I didn't, child. I didn't," Veya replied with a long sigh. Lu was about to argue, but the old woman continued. "But I might as well have. I made many bad decisions."

"Bad decisions? Is that what you call them?" Lu demanded, her voice cutting through the damp night air.

"It's no excuse, but times were hard back then. The Council of Old Women was dominated by ardent Bears–militant isolationists. I spent a year attempting to soften their outlook as drought worsened and enmity with neighbouring settlements grew. We didn't have enough food for the clan, let alone others. I had to walk a fine line to avoid being deposed, but I still made proposals.

"My suggestion to bring food in from the north was countered with ideas of expanding to take over land that didn't belong to us. My idea to offer to escort the settlements' convoys so they could bring supplies south for their needs was rejected."

"But you were Daj! You could give orders."

"The Daj only has the powers the clan grants her, and that gift of trust wanes quickly when the two factions of the clan are in a war of attrition."

"Then why did you leave our crops with so little protection? One warrior clearly was not enough."

"No, it wasn't. But that was at your mother's insistence–"

"You blame my mother?" Lu leapt to her feet and marched across the clearing and stared down into Veya's shelter. She was drenched in seconds, tears mixing with raindrops as she stood panting. Veya uncurled herself from the ball she had huddled in to keep warm and stepped out into the deluge. The old woman squared off an arm's length from Lu and shook off the stoop that had bowed her in recent years. Lu realised the woman she was looking up at had a look of pride on her face.

"Not blame. Credit. I *credit* Tekira with all the good ideas. It was her who knew that I would only shift the clan's politics by getting every Wolf and moderate Bear to the Gathering. It was she that knew the Council would back down if they felt they were under threat of replacement."

Lu's head spun. This was not the history she knew, but she grasped the strategy at play. It sapped at her rage so she threw it aside, not wishing her anger sidetracked.

"Then why was Sofi's help too late?"

"There would never have been help, child. The fields haven't moved. It was a twenty-minute sprint each way then, as it is today."

"Then why didn't we expect the mob to come for our food?" Lu yelled, taking a half-step closer.

"We didn't anticipate that the settlements would attack, girl. But we had planned for it. The agreement was that all of you would run if there was trouble."

"Then why didn't my mother run?" Lu's fists were balled at her sides, and she was yelling at the storm as much as the ex-Daj.

"Because I made some mistakes," Veya yelled back.

"What mistakes?" Lu stepped right up to the old woman and craned her neck to stare into her eyes. She was shocked to see they were brimming.

"I hadn't *ordered* your mother to run. We had agreed it was the best plan, but I hadn't commanded it. I trusted her to do what we had agreed, and I should have known better." Lu's mind reeled and she gulped, for air as much as a meaningful question.

"Why would she stay, then?" was all that came.

"Because the Bears in the clan would expect her to attempt a defence, even if I didn't. A negotiation if nothing else. I bet she didn't want to give the council hardliners an excuse. And she knew two things, child. She knew that once they had food in their bellies, the invaders would think on what they had done and the retribution that might come. They wouldn't repeat that stupidity. And she knew, if things went badly, that her death would be the last straw to shift the council. People would accept . . . demand things must change. She was so popular. I never intended to pass leadership to Ula. It was always your mother. She was meant to be next. It should have been her."

"I can't believe she planned to sacrifice herself, let alone risk her daughter, however brilliant the strategy. There would be a better way."

"You are right, of course. She didn't plan it. When the mob attacked unexpectedly, I believe she tried to negotiate. But somehow it went wrong."

Lu folded her arms around her midsection and stepped back, bent over.

"Is that why you listened to her? Why you let her fool you? Because you worried what she would do when she replaced you?" Lu realised her words weren't fair as she said them. The fire inside her was quickly fading, and her jibe was just bitterness slipping out, with nothing left to hold it back, replaced by the renewed ache of loss.

"No. I had a blind spot with your mother because I loved her. She was younger than me of course, but . . . I truly loved her. Everyone did. But she loved me back. We were . . . very close."

For a while there was no sound. The rain had ceased and neither woman had noticed. Lu startled when the fire spluttered.

"Why have I never heard this? If you knew I had things wrong, why didn't you speak up? Why didn't anyone?"

"Because I'm angry at you!" Veya replied. Her voice cracked as she said it, and Lu looked back to see it was the old woman's turn to ball her fists. "Tekira sacrificed everything for the clan . . . for me . . . but I couldn't be angry at her. She was gone, and I loved her. And she would have run if you weren't hidden in the crevasse. I lost her, partly because she loved you more than me."

"I don't understand."

"She didn't survive, but you did. She would be so ashamed of me if I took my pain out on you, but the joy went out of me, and left an angry, cold void that needs to blame someone. Mostly me, but unfairly, I've also hated the girl, now woman, who I'd loved. I couldn't speak to you about it. Tell you how angry she made me. I avoided you instead."

"Then why choose me to accompany you on this journey?"

"I didn't. Da-Serin is a meddling busybody. And I've already told her so." Veya let out a long breath and the tension seeped from her frame. "But I'm glad she did. I'm glad you met your father. For a man, he's quite the warrior."

"Tell me something of him." Lu didn't think this the time or place, yet part of her needed to hear something other than tragedy.

"She first met him when he got into a fight over his insistence that women in his area earn the same coin as men. He's had so many battles over this that she once joked about leaving the clan to join him. The worthiest war, she used to call it."

Veya's stoop had returned, and she shivered. She began to shuffle back towards her tent.

"I'd like to hear more of my parents. Your version."

"You will, child, you will. But not tonight. And maybe not tomorrow. I've been wrongly angry at you for so long, I can't just put it aside. A stubborn old soul like me needs time." Veya crawled in under her cloak leaving Lu standing alone. Very alone.

Lu took a brand from the fire and used it as a torch to find dry wood deeper under the canopy. When she returned, Veya's snoring was audible from thirty paces. Lu banked the fire for the night and settled under her cloak. Sleep was a long time coming.

When Lu woke, Veya was gone.

Chapter Eleven

Veya could have easily hidden her trail; the fact that she left obvious traces suggested the old woman wanted space but did not want to lose Lu. She left her pony and most of her equipment but had taken her cloak. It seemed she planned to run off her anger and sleep alone.

Lu led the ponies, following at a discreet distance. Occasionally, she would glimpse the woman cresting a rise or across a valley. She would stop for a couple of bells to practice with her sword or fetter their mounts before running up a nearby hill to maintain her stamina.

Veya travelled mostly off-trail, occasionally passing through smallholdings and villages. Once or twice, she followed the main path, and Lu replenished their supplies from passing convoys. Lu was alone, but somehow did not feel it the way she might have a few days ago.

On the third morning, Lu trained, broke camp late, crossed a brook, pushed through a thin line of scrub, and easily picked up Veya's tracks. Soon after eleventh bell, she came upon a well-used deer trail heading south. There was no sign of the old woman on the other side of the path, so Lu turned south. She sped up and kept watch for any sign of Veya returning to the fields. When Lu still had not sighted Veya by noon, she quickened her pace.

When the sun signalled that two more bells had passed, Lu mounted her pony and cantered after the old woman. Half a bell later, she halted, now certain that something was wrong.

Perhaps she grew tired of me following her and hid her tracks. Lu's instincts rejected the thought. Something was seriously wrong. *This is where Mowry would be ideal. I could have kept Veya in sight the whole time.*

Lu tracked better on foot, so she left the ponies untethered by a stream where the grass was lush. They might wander, but she could easily find them again. She took her sword from under the bundle on the pony's side and retrieved her armour from where it had been hidden for weeks in her side pannier. When she had everything in place, she loped off, back the way she had come.

She stopped in several places where fresh human tracks left the deer trail. The first led to a family, camped several hundred strides in a copse of pines. The second showed signs of men with cattle. It soon turned northwest. Dusk was threatening when she found where Veya left the trail. Lu was certain because fifty yards down the narrow path was a dead man with a Mobi'dern blade in his neck.

Veya's sword was still on her pony. This knife would be one she had hidden in the lightweight disguise she wore. The fact that she had not retrieved the knife indicated she had not been able to. The trampled plants and broken twigs suggested Veya had reached this point on her own, but there had been a struggle, and she had been taken. Lu's chest tightened as she considered the possibility—had Veya been taken alive, or was she already dead?

In the failing light, Lu studied the footprints leading away from the trail. At least four men had left, possibly more. It was impossible to tell as they were travelling one behind the other, stepping on each other's footprints. In a few places, she noted deeper prints, likely belonging to someone carrying Veya.

Lu followed until only starlight lit her path. Worried she might miss a turn, she waited for her vision to adjust to the dark, then continued slowly.

The trail led to a steep hill; nearly a cliff face. It was difficult to see very far up in the dark, and she tried to recall how tall the hill had appeared in daylight from afar. The track turned right, and she followed, stopping frequently to listen and look for torches or firelight nearby.

After twenty minutes, the trail split, a side path leading towards a large pile of boulders, that appeared to have fallen in a long-forgotten landslide. Such formations were common in the south, and Lu suspected what she would find behind the mound. She was not disappointed; there was a cavern entrance, hidden by the boulders. Her sharp eyes picked out a glimmer of light from within.

As Lu crept forward, the hairs on the back of her neck rose. She turned and stared back into the darkness, slowly sinking into a crouch with her hand on her sword's grip. Nothing moved, but the night sounds, which had been loud before, had quieted.

A predator.

Her nose tingled as a strong, musky scent reached her. She pictured a bear. There were few animals she feared, but an angry bear with a coat thick enough to dull the bite of her sword was one of them. She checked the wind direction. The smell was coming from the cave, not from behind her, where her instincts screamed the threat lurked.

This must be the bear's lair, but he is out here somewhere, returning from a feed. But that did not make sense. Why was there light coming from the cave? There was only one way to find out.

Splitting her attention between both directions, Lu cautiously ventured toward the hole in the rock face. She eased her head into the doorway. Farther down, around a bend, a torch burned. By its meagre light, she could see bear sign, but it appeared to be very old.

Why does it smell so strongly?

She moved forward to the bend, crouched, and glanced around the corner. The tunnel narrowed just beyond a solitary flame, burning brightly on a tarred stick mounted to the wall. She averted her eyes, preserving her night vision. She unsheathed her sword before venturing into the narrow space, knowing the confined quarters would make it difficult to draw.

With the torch she had taken from the wall now held behind her, Lu could see that the dusty tunnel floor was scuffed, indicating the path was used frequently, and recently. One spot was covered in black marks where other torches had been stored. Whoever had Veya took them to light the way ahead, she surmised.

The air around her cooled as she moved onward. She proceeded slowly, pausing often to listen, fighting the urge to rush and rescue Veya. After what felt like half a bell, a wave of tension suddenly filled her, her body instinctively ready to fight or flee. There was no sound, just the smell of stale air and burning tar. Only twenty or so strides in each direction were visible.

The unsettling thought that someone was creeping up behind her crossed her mind. She spun around, propped the torch against the wall, then moved past it. She sprinted two dozen paces into the darkness, sword raised, and halted in a low, defensive stance. Nothing. But the sense of being stalked lingered.

A burst of rage filled her, followed by an inexplicable sense of victory. She began to wonder if she was losing her mind, or if there were ghosts in the hill, when a muffled sound echoed from the direction of the cave's entrance. It was too distorted to be recognised, but her intuition suggested it was a large beast roaring. She shivered, noting that the strange feelings had ceased. She waited a long five minutes, sensing nothing more, before turning, collecting the torch, and continuing through the tunnel after Veya. Though her focus was on what lay ahead, she kept most of her attention sharply attuned to the tunnel behind her.

Lu stumbled when the tunnel took a sharp turn upward. She sheathed her blade and shifted the torch to her other hand.

A few minutes later, Lu realised she was approaching a light. She propped the torch against the wall once more and crept forward. After a few more careful strides, she heard voices.

Hugging the shadows, Lu made her way toward the glow ahead. The tunnel did not get any taller but widened considerably. Soon, it was light enough to see that the walls had been cut rather than formed naturally. She spotted the entrance to what appeared to be a cavern ahead. Tall enough to walk through near the centre, the ceiling dropped to the left, while the floor rose sharply to the right, as if a giant had slashed diagonally through the rock.

Lu edged up the right side as she approached the opening. At first, she crouched, but then dropped to her knees and crawled into the narrow space near the top, keeping watch for scorpions and spiders. She peeked over the rim of the wall, into a round, bowl-like clearing below.

Lu eased forward and saw they were still far underground. The cavern sat at the base of what must once have been an open-cast mineshaft. Evidence of cave-ins and subsidence had widened the shaft to perhaps fifty paces. Debris had long since been cleared, and a sizable camp had been set up.

Water trickled down the far wall, collecting in large pots beside what appeared to be a kitchen. Lu's oddly sharpened sense of smell detected the latrines before her eyes spotted them in a distant corner. She counted three large tables and low wooden bunks for twenty people.

In a few bells, daylight would flood down from above. For now, a dozen flickering torches overwhelmed any starlight that might have provided more illumination.

A burrow for bandits, no doubt. She could see a dozen men, all armed with at least a dagger, and five wore swords on their belts. Lu scoured the cavern floor twice but could not spot Veya. She watched the men, hoping their movements might reveal where the old woman was hidden.

After minutes of frustration and second-guessing whether she was on the right trail, Lu gasped as the camp suddenly brightened, snapping into sharp focus. It was as if a shadow that had blanketed everything had been lifted. She spotted Veya immediately, bound on a bunk between some barrels, lying on her side. Her left leg was bloody and at an odd angle. Broken. Rage filled Lu, but she pushed it away. Now was not the time for emotion.

A young man sat on the ground by Veya's side, his back against the bunk next to hers. She could see his lips move as he spoke–his face red with anger–but Lu could not catch his words. Yet when she concentrated, they suddenly reached her, distant but clear.

"Pa recognised you when we passed on the road. You didn't know him, despite negotiating many contracts with him when you were clan leader. To you, he was just a nameless trader, but your face is etched in his mind. Your clan killed his wife's brother and two of his own. He always boasted he would get even, even if it took a lifetime . . ."

The words faded for a while, until the man stood and spoke once more.

"He should have been here by now. He went to send a messenger to fetch his wife—he wanted her to see the blood debt paid." The man looked toward the cave entrance, causing Lu to duck back. "I can't think what delayed him. He was fit to cut your eyes out when he went."

Panic surged as Lu gripped the rock in front of her. Though she had ducked back, the scene below remained clear, as if she could still see it. Then the image began to fade. It was like staring at the sun, then closing her eyes and still seeing an outline—only this afterimage was crisp and clear as it dwindled away. She forced herself to study the remaining details, though they made no sense.

Cautiously, she eased forward and looked to where Veya lay, only to realise she could not see the woman. A pile of crates now blocked her view. She shook her head. *They had not been there a moment ago.*

Lu concentrated on the afterimage, and the crates were there, but slightly off to one side. It was as if she was seeing them from the vantage point of someone on the other side of the broad tunnel entrance. She was about to turn when hot breath brushed her cheek. Her hand snapped to her belt knife as she jerked her head around. A stride away, two large yellow eyes and a set of enormous fangs glistened, framed by a mouth smeared with fresh blood. She froze though her heart raced, threatening to burst from her chest.

There was no way to extract her weapon before the beast would be on her.

Dare I even move? She locked eyes with the creature and made her expression as intimidating as possible. But after a dozen rapid heartbeats, she noticed that the creature's tongue was lolling lazily from its mouth, its breathing calm. She had spent enough time with prida to recognise a relaxed beast. The mountain cat licked its lips, snorted quietly, then rolled onto its side, inviting a belly rub.

Chapter Twelve

The shape of the mountain lion's head was familiar. It was difficult to see in the flickering light within the crevice where they lay, but she was sure she knew this animal. The cat extended its right paw, claws retracted, to tap her arm for attention. A small scar from an infected porcupine quill marred its paw, a wound that had not healed well. Lu's breath caught. She recognised the scar–and the young female mountain lion.

Stupid cat? The animal let out a blast of foul-smelling air from her rear end, followed by a deep rumble in her throat. Lu rocked back to take the weight off her left arm and extended her hand to rub the cat's chest.

I have no idea what's going on, or how you got here, but I'm glad you came. Did you bring help? Of course, the cat did not reply.

Before prida are bonded, they are trained in the hand signals used by the Mobi'dern and their animals. The wardens ensure readiness to receive instructions from their chosen warrior long before the pair link minds and create a more effective communication link. Lu gave the cat another scratch, then lifted her hand to give the signal to prepare for attack. The cat responded with silent, eager anticipation.

Lu noticed blood on her hand from the cat's shoulder. *This cat had killed recently.* She scoured her mind to make sense of it and as if in reply, an image formed in her mind: an older man, with a thunderous expression, stomping into the tunnel she had recently traversed. She looked at the cat, who was peering down into the cavern. *The man was coming behind me . . . and you killed him. And I can see it in your mind. It's like a bond-link. But how can–*

The cat suddenly tensed, spinning her head to look back. A moment later, the sound of running feet came from the darkness behind them. *Two pairs of feet.* Lu sank back into the deepest part of the shadowed crevice. She did not worry about the cat; her coat blended perfectly with the shadowed rock.

An old woman, aided by a man in his twenties, passed below. Lu could see them clearly in the sphere of light cast by the torch they carried. The woman wept, calling out.

"Bryndon. Bryn . . ." Lu looked over the edge of the cavern lip and saw the man who had been talking to Veya run to meet the pair.

"We found your Pa back in the tunnel, Bryn," said the man who had arrived with the woman. The woman shook off his helping hand and reached for Veya's tormentor. Her strength left her as she collapsed into him, and he gently lowered her to the ground.

"He's dead, Bryn," the old woman wailed.

"Ravaged by a beast, he was. There was so much blood." A crowd was gathering around them.

"The old crone's animal must be nearby," said one, and all heads swivelled toward the cave's entrance.

They have no reason to delay, and more reason than ever to kill Veya. Soon they will fortify the entrance to fend off the killer in the tunnel. She looked down at the crowd of people, most of whom were unarmed. Lu committed to battle.

She let out a low hiss to get the cat's attention, pointed to where Veya lay, and gave the sign for "protect." The cat did not hesitate. As she bounded away, Lu rolled out of the nook, dropped into a crouch, checked that her three knives were within easy reach, then crept forward.

The cat ignored the men as she streaked past them, but they yelled and scrambled out of her path. Two of the five wearing swords drew them, holding them defensively. Two unarmed men dashed away towards the bunks, presumably to retrieve their weapons. The cat reached Veya, turned, and bared her teeth. Her snarl echoed off the cavern walls. The crowd's attention locked on the snarling cat, giving Lu the opening she needed.

Lu steadied her breath, feeling the familiar weight of her sword in her hand. There was no turning back now. Lu struck. In the first half second, she closed half the distance, and her blade sang against its scabbard's leather as she drew it free. Her eyes darted, selecting targets, while her mind recalled her sponsor's teaching on being heavily outnumbered.

You will think you need to kill many to survive. But injuring is often quicker than a killing stroke. In the first phase of attack, buy yourself time by creating bloody mayhem.

As she reached the back of the crowd, Lu veered left toward the two men with drawn swords who were regaining their senses and inching toward the cat. Her blade flashed, and in a single, swift stroke, its tip tore through the tendons and muscles of the back of three men's legs. She was careful not to let the blade bite deeper; any snag would slow her momentum.

In her next step the sword swung upward, flinging blood into the air. She leaned her weight into the next strike, severing one of the swordsman's hands clean off at the wrist. Pivoting on her right foot, she pulled the blade down, point first, driving it into the thigh of the other man brandishing a weapon. Five men were out of the fight before the first even began to react to her presence. Cries of pain erupted as the injured men crumpled to the ground, clutching at their wounds.

Out of the corner of her eye, she saw a man by a bunk, fumbling in his panic to arm a crossbow. But in moments, he would have the advantage. With her free hand, she signed for the cat to eliminate that threat. Once again, the cat did not hesitate, dropping low and sneaking around the bunk where Veya lay. The old woman was already pulling herself to her feet despite her bonds.

The man two strides from Lu, who had just begun to draw his dagger from a wrist sheath, was the next threat. Lu stepped into him, placing a foot behind his, and tripped him onto his back. As he fell, she considered slashing her blade across his throat but then spotted another man freeing his sword from its scabbard. Her mind registered it was Bryndon. She would drive her blade through his heart, then withdraw, pivot, and fall back to protect the now-exposed Veya. She lunged toward him, her sword arcing back the other way before looping high over her head to gain momentum, whistling as it sliced through the air.

"Halt!" Veya's word was sharp and crisp, with the tone used in the training matt'e. It grabbed Lu's attention. She reacted instinctively, diverting her blade the moment before it penetrated Bryn's chest. She bled off its energy by twirling it once around her body. Pivoting to her right, she guided the sword up, over her shoulder, and down into its scabbard. Her turn brought her neatly in front of Veya, facing the men. A knife had appeared in her raised left hand, while her right hand flowed out, low, and forward, as she sank down into Ninth Stance.

Lu held her body perfectly still, but her senses were everywhere. The men in agony in front of her. Veya grunting as she put weight on her broken leg, stumbling and catching herself on a musty barrel. The crossbowman finally getting a bolt into the track, raising the weapon-only to have a brown blur streak up from behind and smash into him. The trigger snapped, the string twanged, and the arrow shot harmlessly toward the back of the cavern.

Veya whistled two quick tones, and the cat backed several strides away from the man, who was curled into a ball, his weapon beside him.

"She will attack you if you move," Veya called to the crossbowman. To the men in front of Lu, she said, "And Lu will kill any of you who reach for a weapon." As the room quieted, Lu realised she was covered in blood, some of it trickling down her face. She knew it was not hers, but that was all. She ignored it, holding her position as if she were a statue. One of the men was bolder than the others.

"If we all move together, we can–"

"No, you can't," Veya snapped. "She *will* kill you."

Veya shuffled forward to Lu's side, leaving plenty of space for Lu to react if needed. She extended her bound hands toward the older woman still sitting on the floor, her tone softening.

"Hasn't there been enough blood? If not, you can have mine." The woman looked up at her, her mouth falling open.

"I'm so sorry about your husband," Veya continued gently. "But I give you your son's life. Your husband and Bryn kidnapped me and broke my leg. Most would die for doing less to an ex-Daj. Today's blood accounting is balanced, though it may not feel that way to you, I'm sure.

"But your hatred stems from my past actions, and that account has been outstanding too long. The droughts drove us all to make mistakes, but I'm responsible for mine, and I likely owe a blood debt. So, if you need more blood . . . take mine."

Lu could not believe what she was hearing and glanced over at Veya. A subtle twitch of Veya's hand signalled her to remain still. Lu returned to watching for threats, focusing on settling her breathing.

"But if you want it," Veya continued, speaking to the woman on the floor, "*you* must take it. No one will stop you. But it must be you who does it, to balance the debt." Bryn put his hand on the hilt of his belt knife.

"Or him," Veya added, her eyes on Bryn. "If that was his father."

"I was coming to stop it," the old woman on the floor found her voice. "Arranon's anger turned him inward. It drove him to the bottle, for a time, and it took much to dry him out. It left him hollow, but after years of sorrow, he found his joy again. If he'd killed you today, I would have lost him all over again. I came to stop him."

Bryn dropped to his mother's side. "Ma, shouldn't we–"

"Your Pa did bad things in the drought days, too, Bryn. His hatred wasn't all for the Mobi'dern. Much of it was for himself, for his own actions. You've never killed, son. Don't follow him down that dark path."

"Again, I'm sorry for today's death," Veya said. "And I'll offer one last time, my blood is yours if it settles the score. I won't offer another time. We will walk away, and this will be over."

Lu watched Bryn's inner struggle play out on his face. His mother gripped his arm.

"When she offered me the gift of your life, Bryn, she wasn't talking about that young warrior's blade. She was talking about your soul. Your peace. A lifetime outside the bottle, not trapped within it. Think of your own wife and children."

Bryn's eyes unfocused, drifting away from Veya's face as he imagined his family. His body slowly sagged, and he looked toward his mother.

"Go," he whispered in a croaky voice.

At Veya's signal, Lu stood and cut the ropes binding the ex-Daj's hands and feet. Veya reached down beside the barrel and picked up a short staff, tucking it under her arm as a crutch. She took a step toward the tunnel.

"What about what she did to my men?" one of the others asked.

"You are bandits. Your blood is mine to take any time I wish," Veya replied in a tone so chilling that Lu shivered. The man stepped aside.

Veya extended an arm to Lu, who slipped under it to take some of the old woman's weight.

"Call your cat," Veya said. Lu whistled three times, and the cat bounded after them as they left.

Chapter Thirteen

Navigating the tunnel had been difficult with Veya's injuries, and she was spent by the time they reached a small clearing near the entrance. Lu left the cat to protect her, fetched the ponies, and diverted to a nearby smallholding to rent a cart. It took most of the day.

After the adrenaline rush of the rescue and stresses of helping the ex-Daj set her injuries, Lu was grateful for some time alone. She had a lot to process. She catalogued her many questions, yet the feelings coming across her link to the cat drew her back to her unexpected bonding. How did she feel about it? She was thrilled to be bonded—especially as she had worried so recently that she might not be chosen. Now she worried that a premature bonding might have issues she had never considered. And a cat, not an eagle? What about her dreams?

She approached the subject from a few angles: cataloguing the pros and cons, listening to her gut, and reflecting on how Mowry and the cat had interacted over the past months—the former aloof and distant, the latter curious and occasionally flatulent. There was a shift in her feelings. Did it matter what she had dreamt of? There is a power in being chosen. Even when she was six years old, she recalled the Blade stepping forward to sponsor her. It had been more than just a practical solution to a problem. She was wanted, and that mattered. She had felt the bond form with the woman, a woman she had only seen from a distance.

When she returned to the clearing, it was dark. Veya had sent the cat to hunt, and two rabbits now hung on a spit over a small fire.

As they ate, they talked, and Lu asked all the questions about her father that had clouded her mind for days. Veya answered each one openly. She thought him a good man, but just a man, nonetheless. Lu asked his name, Veya told her. It had a good feel on her tongue as she repeated it.

"We need to do something about your bond-mate here," Veya said, pointing to the sleeping cat sprawled out in front of the fire.

"How did I bond before the trials?" Lu asked.

"It's rare, but there is no reason you can't bond at any time, aside from the traditions and practices we keep in place. Your mother did it, you know. It was the last time I recall it happening."

"The prida always chooses," Lu said.

"Always. Are you disappointed? I heard you wanted Mowry."

"I did, I guess. But how useful would he have been in the tunnel? He wouldn't have stopped the bowman for long, either. And I think I tracked you better in the dark because the cat was lending me her senses."

"Yes, your senses will be sharpening, and you'll also experience the world through what she senses. In return, she will gain greater intelligence, language, and other things from you. Now, lay down and get some sleep. You haven't rested in two days. You'll sleep deeply. I'll keep watch and I promise to be here in the morning. Now that the link has formed, you'll exchange much with your prida as you rest. Enjoy it. I still hold memories of mine tightly."

Lu ran her fingers through her hair and looked at her cat. She lay back and was asleep in moments.

Chapter Fourteen

Lu knew she was dreaming by the context of the world surrounding her-memories shared by the cat. Scenes came and went, with new images pressed on her: offerings of food, a desire for play and grooming, and the urge to hunt side by side.

Lu had pestered Lore and her wardens for knowledge about the transformation bonding brought and knew this was how language formation began. *Treating it like play works best,* she recalled Lore's advice. She pressed the name of each offering back towards the cat and added some of her own ideas into the game.

As soon as you can, offer your prida its name. Lu remembered asking Lore how the names are chosen.

"Mowry is an example of a name that seems to fit the animal, so we all use it. During the bonding, that name will probably stick, but it's also common for a new name to emerge. The name will feel right in the moment. But other animals don't gain a name before bonding. Again, the right name will arrive at the right moment."

I can't call you Stupid Cat, Lu thought, struck by a pang of guilt for having used that name for such a glorious animal. She pushed the feeling away.

My father is called "Shannak." It's a good name, don't you think? Amid the flow of images and memories coming from the sleeping cat came a response: *Shanna.*

Chapter Fifteen

Approaching Mobi without being spotted by several avian prida is difficult. A healer and six other warriors ran out to meet Veya, Lu, and Shanna, intercepting them several miles from home. As the healer replaced the dressings on Veya's wounds, Lu excused herself to return Shanna to the Wildings' Hollow.

She found Lore and Blade chatting casually outside the Hollow's feed store. Da-Serin was never casual about anything, leading Lu to conclude she was there to discover what had happened to Veya.

Then why look for me here? Perhaps she knows about Shanna. Lore certainly would have noticed her absence.

Mowry sat perched on a post near Lore's shoulder. Lu felt a twinge of longing for her old dreams and a pang of guilt for abandoning them. Shanna bounded forward and leapt up at the eagle, who flapped off with an undignified squawk.

"Then it's true," Lore said with a chuckle. She turned to the cat and said, "You've claimed your warrior. Did she name you Stupid Cat?"

Lu's face flushed, and she looked at her feet.

"Shanna. Her name is Shanna. After my father." The cat circled and sniffed Lore's hand, hoping for a treat, but flopped down unsatisfied with a snort in front of Lu, who bent to pet her.

"Sounds like you've had an adventure. Report!" the Blade barked.

Lu shot to her feet and gave a concise account of events. Veya had sworn Lu to silence about their arguments, grinning as she remarked that this would frustrate Da-Serin, but it was not her business. Lu briefly mentioned meeting her father and focused on Veya's kidnapping, the rescue, and Shanna's unexpected arrival.

"I assigned you to protect Veya, so why weren't you at her side when she was taken?" the Blade asked. Her words were chiding, but her tone gave Lu the impression she already knew the reason.

"Er . . . Veya wanted some time alone, so I followed at a distance." The Blade huffed at the reply but did not press the issue. Instead, she smiled, and, in a rare public display of affection drew Lu into an awkward hug. Then, she bent and stroked Shanna's flank, before leaving to brief the Daj.

Lore stepped closer, placing a hand on each of Lu's shoulders. She looked her up and down, as if she could see some difference since the bonding.

She probably can, Lu admitted to herself.

"Anyway, I'm sorry she ran away," Lu said. "Although I'm glad she found us, of course. I've brought her back to Wildings' Hollow." Lu's tone was heavy with sadness–she had grown close to the cat on the trail home and would miss her. "I assume there is some training she needs before the trials."

"No, now that she has chosen her bond-mate she will fight with the other prida candidates. She can't stay here." Lore laughed when Lu's face lit up, breaking into a huge grin.

Lu spent a bell with Lore, explaining how the connection had developed over the past few days and learning about the challenges Shanna would face as she integrated with the other mature prida. At the end of the impromptu lesson, Lu asked the questions that had been on her mind for the past few days.

"I didn't know prida could bond before the trials. How did Shanna choose me when I was so far from home?"

"It happened before you left, Lu. I saw the signs but wasn't certain, so I didn't act. And yes, it is rare."

"Veya says my mother bonded early." Lore smiled. Lu felt a familiar sadness at speaking of her mother but noticed it was far lighter than she was accustomed to. As the emotion passed through her, Shanna raised her head and nuzzled Lu's hand.

Thank you, she sent. Over the past few days, Lu and Shanna had established almost two dozen words and phrases they both consistently understood.

A young girl ran up to them with a message, summoning them both to the Dajmut. Lu's stomach fluttered with concern.

Come, she sent. She could have used hand signs but enjoyed opening and closing the mental connection, savouring the warmth that flooded though it.

Minutes later, Lu stood at attention, surrounded by the Council of Old Women, who encircled her with a ritualistic air. Outside, Shanna grumbled at being left with the other prida, who had each raised their hackles or shown other signs of challenge until Lore barked a word Lu did not recognise.

"The Blade has shared the report of your mission as has Veya," Daj-Ula said. "You performed well." It was not the clan's way to offer overt praise, so Lu stood taller upon hearing these words, knowing they carried weight.

"You have your pins, and your prida, but I will not elevate you to warrior status until you acquit yourself honourably at the trials." Lu had wondered about this but did not dare ask. She felt a bit disappointed but had not expected to be elevated yet. "You will pass, I'm certain, but be mindful; you've already begun to rely on your bond-mate. You won't have her when facing K'Tang and the others. You will need to adjust to using *only* your own senses, not yours and the cat's. Switching back and forth seamlessly is a skill we all had to learn, but we didn't face the trials immediately after bonding."

"Thank you," Lu said. "I have no expectation of special treatment, of course, and will be diligent in my preparations."

"It doesn't appear that way," the Blade replied, her tone sharp. Lu could not think of what she had done to offend but immediately tightened her stance and stared straight ahead. "When did it become acceptable to attend a meeting with the Council of Old Women improperly dressed?"

Lu risked a glance down at her outfit. She had straightened everything and raked a hand through her hair as they walked from the Hollows.

"My apologies," Lu said. "I'm not sure–"

"Give me your sword. And take off that armour!" Blade barked. Lu quickly unclipped her scabbard ties and reached behind in the proper ritualistic manner to draw her sheathed sword around her body, as she would in a formal ceremony. She held it horizontally at shoulder height, arms extended, until Da-Serin relieved her of it. Then she scrambled to remove her leathers, folding them neatly on the floor in front of her. Her mind felt Shanna's concern. She pushed comforting thoughts back in return, even though she felt far from relaxed.

Lu resumed the attention position, feeling naked, despite wearing the clan's novice clothing she had changed to on the final leg of their journey, after discarding the disguise.

"You must complete the trials, Lu," Daj-Ula said, "but we've decided that your recent actions, and the fact that the best prida candidate in a generation already deems you worthy, warrants recognition." The Daj turned, taking a bundle from a bench behind her. "Here is the first set of warrior clothing you crafted. Change into it when you return to the new hut we've assigned you, and wear it with pride for a lifetime."

Lu's throat tightened, and she could barely utter her thanks as she accepted the uniform. Its colours seemed brighter than she remembered them.

"And you will need this," the Blade said, holding out a sword and scabbard. "A warrior doesn't carry a third-rank sword. This one of the fifth rank was your mother's." Lu's eyes locked onto the weapon in the Blade's hands, and she did not hear the rest of the woman's sentence. Her hands trembled as she reached for it, but she steadied them with her will. The urge to ease the blade from its beautiful leather scabbard was powerful, but instead, she forced herself through the ritual moves, swinging the weapon in an elegant arc around her body and securing it on her back. She would spend hours later fine-tuning and adjusting the straps.

For now, Lu focused on keeping the tears from her eyes and resumed her position at attention. A moment later, she was at a loss for what to do when all seven clan leaders relaxed, stepped forward, and hugged her.

Chapter Sixteen

Lu became aware of the heat and dampness on her face as she slowly swam back to consciousness from a dream. She had been reliving her epic encounter with K'Tang in the trials, now two moons behind her. Each bout had been lengthy, and Lu was proud she won two; the crowd had expected K'Tang to win all five. The look of pride on Da-Serin's face would live in her memory forever.

The fierce dreams must have caused night-sweats, Lu thought-just a fraction of a second before realising Shanna's warm, wet tongue was the cause.

Wake, the boy approaches, sent the cat.

Each newly minted warrior had been assigned a mission, as per the clan's tradition. Lu's assignment was typical–a convoy escort in a relatively low risk part of the nation, intended to build her sense of worth, independence, and confidence. She was in northern Quartt, escorting wheat wagons from the farms of Pillum up to the snowy wastes in the Northern Region, where food is scarce.

On the sixth day of their ride north, they passed through the village of Mecklemead and were approached by the local justice. At his request, the convoy took on a widower and his young son. The man, a retired soldier who had been serving as the village sheriff, had fallen from his horse, suffering a severe head injury. After two moons, the local healer believed he would never recover. His scant savings had dwindled, and the justice needed him, and his six-year-old son delivered to the man's two sisters, who lived a hundred miles to the north. It was on the convoy's route.

Lu rolled onto her feet as the man's son, Gord, rounded the rock she had spent the night behind. He was red-faced and panting for breath from the climb up the short hill. The convoy was camped in the pass below, while Lu slept on higher ground-a better vantage point. Shanna also disturbed the horses less at a distance, ensuring everyone rested well through the night.

"Pa's wandered off in the night," he blurted out. "I tied string to his ankle and mine, like I always do, but it snagged on a rock and snapped while I slept. I've run around searching, but there's no sign of him."

Lu looked the boy over. The pre-dawn light revealed his brave little face, pale with worry. He carried a dagger in his belt–long enough to be a short sword on his small frame–and a man's spear that had been cut in half. Over the last two days, Shanna had taken an interest in him, so Lu, who had little time for children, had become more acquainted with him. Annoyingly, he latched onto her, eager to become a warrior like his father had been before his accident. He took pains to show her his techniques, which she patiently helped him improve.

"You went running around in the forest? At night?" Lu said. She was not cross; she was impressed with his courage.

"I hoped your cat might track him?" Gord asked, sheepishly.

Lu showed him the hand sign for "track" while mentally sharing the task with Shanna. When the boy gave the cat the signal, she sighed, then bounded away, with Gord on her heels. Lu jogged along behind, shaking off the last of the fog from her sudden awakening.

Shanna circled the camp, staying clear of the area where the horses were tethered, until she picked up the father's scent. As they ventured deeper into the forest, Lu stopped Gord several times to show him the trace marks his father had left, patiently teaching him the basics of tracking.

"Learn this well, Gord. You may lose him again and not have Shanna's nose to help you."

The sun was well up when Shanna shared that she sensed the man ahead, over a rise, behind some trees. He lingered near fast-running water. Lu grasped the boy's hand and began to lead him forward, but Shanna stepped into her, blocking her path with her body.

Let the cub lead the hunt, she sent. *Look, he sees the sign.* The cat was right. Lu watched as the six-year-old used his spear to push aside a low branch and study an imprint partially hidden below. She had taught him to use something other than his hand in case snakes or spiders lurked in the foliage. Lu had not seen the print herself, as she had been relying on Shanna's nose. They hung back as the boy advanced, taking his time, concentrating on every square inch he passed.

"Pa!" he yelled when he caught sight of his father's back. The man was sitting on the edge of a river, soaking his feet. Gord ran up and hugged him before reprimanding him for wandering off. His father looked sad and confused but did not react. Instead, he shared a tale about fishing in a similar stream to feed his military unit on a long march.

Lu ate with the convoy's leader, discussing the next leg of their route. Afterward, she loped off to find Shanna, who was already scouting for trouble ahead. They each took a side of the road, far enough from it to flank anyone hiding and posing a threat. They were out of sight of each other, but their mental link remained open and warm.

You were smart to let the boy find his father back there, Lu sent, adding the warmth of her pride for her bond-mate.

The cub is young but fierce. He will grow to be alpha, guarding his father and taking a mate of his own.

Lu reflected on how Shanna's thoughts and ideas complemented her own. Prida are trained to be independent fighting partners, not pets or servants, and Lu embraced how their union enhanced her own decision-making and helped keep her trust issues at bay.

I believed I was strong before we bonded, she sent. *You've helped me become more mature and well-rounded. Have I helped you, too?* She winced at how needy her question sounded.

Lu had begun to understand her cat had a strong sense of play, which she now recognised across their link as Shanna replied.

Yes. When I corner a porcupine, I find you extremely useful.

What's next?

Thank you for reading *Bonds of Ascension*, a *Weavers of Destiny* novella. I hope you loved the journey as much as I loved writing it.

Enjoyed the Book?

Please consider leaving a review—even just a few lines—on Amazon, Goodreads, or your preferred platform. Reviews help other readers discover stories they'll love, and they mean the world to authors.

Read the Complete Duology

The *Weavers of Destiny* duology is now complete and ready for you to explore at www.andrewplatten.com/books

Book One: *Strands of Time and Magic*
Book Two: *Chains of Fear and Fury*

More from the World of Mordeland

Webs of Treason, a companion novella, is available at www.andrewplatten.com/books

Stay Connected

Visit www.andrewplatten.com to sign up for early access to stories, behind-the-scenes extras, and exclusive offers.

Acknowledgements

The original concept for the first book in the Weavers of Destiny series, Strands of Time and Magic—a tale about Levinial, the time weaver—took an unexpected turn for the better. First, the characters of Brylee and Lu quickly took control of the plot, steering the story in unexpected directions. I shouldn't have been surprised, as my circle of female friends is driven, intelligent, and accomplished. I'm fortunate to be surrounded by such inspiring women who have shaped the strength and depth of the characters in my story.

The second improvement—unsurprisingly, for anyone who knows us—came over a drink at the pub, when I first shared the plot with my wife, Darielle. After listening thoughtfully, she asked, "And where are the animal companions?" Thus, the Mobi'dern and their prida were born. It wasn't until this novella and Chains of Fear and Fury, the second book in the series, that the clan truly came to life.

I would be remiss not to thank Darielle for reading through the novella several times as alpha reader, beta reader, and editor.

Andrew Tsui, Mike Hrycyk, and Olivia Hawthorne served as advance readers for Strands of Time and Magic and later provided invaluable feedback as alpha readers for this novella. Your insights and support have helped make both books stronger—thank you!

Karen Slade, thank you for being an alpha reader for Bonds of Ascension. Your enthusiasm and support for my stories means more than you know.

Lastly, thank you to all the authors who write inspirational novels featuring fierce female warriors and brave animal companions. Bagheera in The Jungle Book and Guenhwyvar in the Drizzt series, Rothfuss's Adem and Hobb's Mountain Queen in her Farseer trilogy to name a few. I've enjoyed bringing my own version to life, creating the society and its governance model, as well as the 'science' and mysticism of the bonding process behind warrior and prida.

About the Author

Born in England, I emigrated to Canada with my two children and now live in the Comox Valley on Vancouver Island.

My initial career was in technology; a realm akin to magic with its ability to make lives better (and worse). It has mystery, a language few can master, and often fails us just when we need it most. It's no surprise to me that many who revel in fantasy are drawn from the ranks of technology.

I am a view junkie and am drawn to places where I can imagine being an explorer discovering them for the first time. It's why I became a pilot. People-watching is also one of my favourite hobbies. I try to understand how our minds, perceptions, and emotions work. The hundreds of hours of podcasts and papers I devour don't make me a psychology expert, but they have helped me develop the characters that act out the book's plot.

Oh, and I am tormented by cheese. I love cheese.

Learn more about me, my work, events, and access bonus content at www.andrewplatten.com

www.ingramcontent.com/pod-product-compliance
Lightning Source LLC
Chambersburg PA
CBHW020557130626
46552CB00007B/2926